The Weight of Blood

by David Dalglish

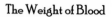

BOOKS BY DAVID DALGLISH

THE HALF-ORC SERIES

The Weight of Blood
The Cost of Betrayal
The Death of Promises
The Shadows of Grace
A Sliver of Redemption

THE WORLD OF DEZREL

A Dance of Cloaks
Guardian of the Mountain

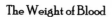

1

The two brothers were almost to the wall when the skulls flew overhead.

"Make them stop!" cried Harruq Tun, hands pressed against his ears. Beside him, Qurrah Tun stood mesmerized by the sight. Hundreds of skulls bathed in purple fire sailed over the walls of Veldaren like dark comets. Gaping mouths shrieked mindless wails, their voices bone-chilling and unrelenting. A few soldiers fired arrows, but most hid behind their shields.

"Why do you cower?" Qurrah asked, striking his brother on the shoulder. "The skulls are nuisances, nothing more."

"Sorry," Harruq muttered. He shivered as a skull sailed just above them, its screech turning to chaotic laughter. The sound raced up and down his spine, triggering fear no matter how irrational.

Qurrah watched as if immune to the sound. He was so much smaller than Harruq, his slender body wrapped in rags, thin flesh clinging to bone. Yet he was unafraid. Shame and embarrassment burned in Harruq's cheeks. He towered over his brother, his hands beefy and arms muscular. Nothing should scare him. He was supposed to be Qurrah's protector, not the other way around.

"Where can we climb?" Harruq asked, hoping to get his mind off the skulls.

"There," Qurrah pointed. A narrow set of stairs climbed to the parapet and Harruq led the way. The city gates were lost in the distance, city guards clustered about them.

"Look," Harruq said. "Orcs."

He spoke the word with an odd reverence, but they both understood its significance. Unlike the humans, the two brothers' skin was dark and tinged with gray, their ears long and curled to a point. They were half-orcs, condemned for the tainted blood coursing through their veins. The people of Veldaren hurled the word at them like a dagger, but in truth neither had ever seen a full orc before.

"Now we'll finally see," Qurrah said, "what we are, what we are meant to be."

Thousands of orcs spilled into the west, needing no light to see in the darkness. They howled and cheered, drums and war chants mixing with the shrieks of the skulls. Harruq felt his temples throb. A wail rolled over him as a deathly comet swirled about, spotting the two and eying them like prey. Try as he might, he couldn't stop from shaking.

"Can you stop them?" Harruq asked, squinting at the sky.

"Perhaps," said Qurrah, eyes distant and unfocused. "But orcs don't use necromancy, not if the stories I've heard are true. Someone else travels with them—someone who must be strong."

"When it comes to this mind stuff, no one's stronger than you."

Qurrah chuckled.

"We'll see."

He closed his eyes, letting his mind sink into the ether. Like scent to a bloodhound, Qurrah could sense the magic flowing all about him. The flame surrounding the skulls flared even brighter, but beneath their tails trailed long threads of silver. When Qurrah looked up, he saw hundreds of the threads twisting and curling together, coiling toward a hidden presence deep within the orc army. Taking in a deep breath, Qurrah pooled his strength and focused on the skull taunting his brother, visualizing the thread and seeking to sever it.

There was a pull on his chest—the taste of copper on his tongue. When he opened his eyes, the skull fell to the battlements. The jaw snapped and rotting teeth clattered to the streets below.

"You did it!" Harruq picked up the skull, frowning at its ordinariness. Shrugging, he flung it toward the distant army of orcs.

"Not done yet," Qurrah said, sweat lining his face, his breathing soft and ragged. "There're so many. So…many…"

He closed his eyes. This time, he didn't grab just one thread. He grabbed them all. They screeched and twisted in his grip. His head pounded, and the pull on his chest was great he felt he might pitch over the wall to his death. Qurrah's well of magic drained at frightening speed. He almost let go, but he thought of his brother, shaking under the spell of the skulls.

No, he thought. *Enough. Cease your chatter.*

He clutched tighter, the threads braiding into a giant rope in his mind. High above, the skulls quieted, and their fires dimmed.

When the necromancer noticed Qurrah's meddling, his mental link pulsed with incredible energy. Colors swarmed through his mind, dark purples and reds across a macabre canvas of black. He felt his chest tightening, his neck constricting. A scrying eye was upon him, now, and he was losing. It felt like an arrow pierced his mind, and through it words seeped into his head.

Run. Die. Collapse. Fear. Failure.

An apparition swirled before him, blacker than the shadows, red eyes smoldering. Its rank claws touched his face, turning the sweat on his brow to ice. The arrow squirmed deeper. Qurrah focused every bit of his will upon it, desperately seeking to repulse it. His well of energy, which he'd thought empty, burgeoned and overflowed. The arrow snapped, banishing the necromancer's presence, but leaving a solitary impression squatting at the back of Qurrah's mind:

Curiosity.

Qurrah opened his eyes. He lay on his back in his brother's arms, yet he didn't remember falling.

"You're alright!" Harruq hugged him.

Qurrah laughed.

"He lost," he said, pointing to the night sky. "And he doesn't know how badly."

One by one, the skulls' fire went out and they fell like morbid hail upon the city.

"Limitless," Qurrah said, his smile trembling. Blood ran from his nose, and his skin was so pale Harruq could see his veins. "The well is limitless."

His eyes rolled into his head. Without another word, he collapsed.

He dreamt of fire poured into flesh and a man whose eyes were glass.

><><

"Qurrah!" Harruq shouted when his brother finally opened his eyes.

"How long?" Qurrah asked as he lurched onto his feet.

"Not long," Harruq said, holding Qurrah's shoulder to steady him. "The orcs are almost here."

As if on cue, they heard a collective roar from the south. Harruq glanced at the stairs along the wall, but Qurrah saw this and shook his head.

"We need to get closer to the fight," Qurrah said, slurring his words. "I need to see him."

"Sure thing," Harruq agreed. "Come on. I have an idea."

He grabbed Qurrah's arm and hooked his elbow around it. Qurrah was too weak to complain, so together they ran down the streets. They passed closed homes containing people praying for safety and victory. Looming ahead of them was the southern gate. Hundreds of soldiers stacked against it, their shields braced and ready. All along the walls, archers released arrow after arrow into the darkness.

"How are we to get closer?" Qurrah asked.

"Ignore them," Harruq said. "I know what I'm doing."

He led them into an alley in between several worn buildings made of stone. He stopped just before the next set of homes, for he heard talking. Holding Qurrah back, he peered around the corner to find a soldier dressed in finely polished armor raising his sword in salute. At first Harruq did not see who he saluted, but an elf fell from the roof and landed before the soldier.

"An elf," Harruq whispered, managing to grab Qurrah's attention. Now both peered around the corner, curious why such an exotic creature had arrived mere seconds before war.

"Greetings, Dieredon," the soldier hailed, pulling off his helmet. He was a middle-aged, blond-haired man who had numerous scars on his face.

"Greetings to you as well, guard captain Antonil," Dieredon said, taking a step back and kneeling. "Though I fear greetings is all I may offer you."

Antonil pointed to the wall, and he asked something which neither could hear when the orc army shouted another communal roar.

"The Ekreissar will not aid you," Dieredon said when the noise died. He shook his head, and a bit of sadness crossed his face. "We have been forbidden. Ceredon insists this is a minor skirmish, nothing more. We are not the keepers of man."

"Minor skirmish?" Antonil shouted. "What about the necromancer traveling with them? You're the one who said he was dangerous, that he might be…"

Another communal roar, even closer.

"I know," Dieredon glared. "Forgive me, Antonil. I will watch, and I will pray. Whoever started this war will not go unpunished."

The elf whistled, and to the brothers' surprise a winged horse landed on the rooftop of a nearby home. Its skin and mane were sparkling white. Dieredon bowed one last time and then leapt into the air, using the ledge of a window to swing himself onto the roof. He mounted his horse, patted her side, and then took off into the night.

"Damn it all!" Antonil shouted, slamming his mailed fist into the wall. Still shaking his head, he stormed back to the gate, muttering curses.

"What was that all about?" Harruq asked.

"King Vaelor asked for aid and the elves declined," Qurrah answered, chuckling. "The King's pride will not take too kindly to that."

"He and his pride can suck a rotten egg," Harruq said. "Hurry or we'll miss the battle."

He pulled his brother down the alley to where a tall, crumbled house leaned near the wall.

"Onto my shoulders," Harruq suggested, grabbing Qurrah's knees and hoisting him high. Qurrah latched onto the roof, paused, and then stepped onto Harruq's shoulders. The extra height boosted his head and chest above the roof, allowing him to climb to the top despite a moment of flailing. Harruq clapped for him, and he smiled at the next roar from the orcs. It was a goofy smile, and Qurrah recognized the fear hiding behind it.

"Hurry," Qurrah said as Harruq climbed, using a windowsill as a foothold. Together, they stood upon the roof and gazed over the wall, mesmerized by the sight before them. Mere seconds away, hundreds and hundreds of orcs charged. Their race could see as well in night as in day. That same racial ability allowed the two brothers to watch the approaching orcs, lean muscle bulging underneath their sweat-glistened pale gray skin. Some wore mismatched armor, though most had only skulls, straps of leather, and war paint covering their bodies.

Wave after wave of arrows rained upon them, and those who fell were trampled by the rest, but the masses were not even slowed. Harruq pointed past the army to where a long line of men stood in the distance, carrying no light or torch.

"What are they doing?" he asked.

Qurrah searched the line, and he saw what he suspected.

"The necromancer," he observed, pointing to the black shape hidden underneath robes and a hood. "Those alongside him are dead, Harruq. They serve only him."

"Huh," Harruq said. "Lot of good he's doing. How are the orcs going to get through the wall, they have nothing but…"

The man in black robes lifted his hand. Qurrah saw pale and bony fingers hooked in strange formations. Then came the fire, erupting as if those fingers were a crack releasing the melted rock of the abyss. The sudden light blinded them both. The fire burned through the orcs as a solid beam, melting their bodies and scattering their remains. When it struck the wooden gate, it exploded. Wood shattered. Guards behind the gate howled as molten rock struck them, piercing through their shields and armor.

The orcs roared at the sight, not at all upset at their own losses. The way into the city was clear. Axes and swords held high, they rushed the opening.

"A minor skirmish," Qurrah chuckled, echoing the elf's words. "How amusingly wrong."

Harruq had anticipated watching the fight over the wall from the roof, but instead they turned and watched the orcs slam into the human forces that surrounded the opening. The first push was brutal. Screams of pain and the sound of clashing of metal on metal flowed into the city. Harruq watched an orc wielding two swords cut off the arm of one soldier, and, as the blood from the limb splattered across his face, he turned and decapitated another with two vicious hacks. The orc roared in victory only to die as a soldier shoved his sword in his side and out his back.

"Will they make it through?" Harruq asked, in awe of the display. Qurrah glanced over the wall and then back to the main combat. Archers continued eviscerating the orc forces. If they could push into the city, their arrows would be a nuisance at best, but it seemed they had underestimated the human soldiers.

"They are running out of time," Qurrah said. "But they might."

He glanced back to the necromancer, and then he saw his eyes, just hints of red underneath the hood of his robes. Qurrah shivered as whispers shot up his spine.

You silenced my pets, it said.

"I do as I wish," Qurrah whispered back. He felt a touch of cold on his fingers, like the fleeting kiss of a corpse lover.

You ally with the city of men?

"Again, I do as I wish," Qurrah whispered.

"Who are you talking to?" Harruq asked. "Qurrah, what's going on?"

"Nothing," Qurrah said. He tore his gaze back to the fight. More orcs had pushed inward, leaving them bunched in a wide circle. They flung themselves against the surrounding guards. Again he felt a cold chill, this time creeping across his arms like frost spiders. The sensation of being watched was unbearable.

"We need to move," he said. "If the guards falter we might suffer."

"We're already high up," Harruq said. "We're perfectly safe…"

"I said now!" Qurrah shouted. He doubled over, hacking and coughing. His breath was raspy and weak. "Please," he insisted. "Take me from the wall." "Alright then," Harruq said, grabbing his brother's arm. "Just hold tight."

He leapt off the roof, pulling Qurrah with him. As his feet smacked the hard ground, his knees buckled and he fell back, catching his brother as he did. Without a word of thanks, Qurrah stepped off him and leaned against the wall. His whole body shuddered. He had often looked into the darkness. For the first time, the darkness had looked back, and it was amused. Whoever this necromancer was, Qurrah knew he had been an idiot to challenge him.

"Lead the way," Qurrah said. "And forgive my outburst."

"I understand," Harruq said, ignoring the pain in his knees and the bit of blood running from his elbow to his wrist. "We need to hurry, though."

He looped his arm through Qurrah's and then hurried down the alley. As a soldier's body collapsed at the end, the two stopped, and Harruq swore.

"The orcs made it through," he said, to which Qurrah nodded. "This could be bad."

An orc stepped into the alley, blood splashed across his gray skin. He held a sword in each hand, dripping gore coating both. Shouting something in a guttural language neither understood, the orc charged.

"Get back," Harruq ordered as he shoved Qurrah to one side. He slammed himself against a house, barely dodging a downward chop of the blades. The orc attacked again, all his strength behind the swing. Harruq ducked, narrowly avoiding decapitation. Qurrah lunged before the orc could strike again, latching onto his wrist and letting dark magic flow. The orc howled at the sensation of a hundred scorpions stinging his flesh. Flooded with adrenaline, he hurled Qurrah aside, desperate to break the contact between them. Qurrah's thin body crumpled against the dirt. At the sight of it, Harruq felt his rage break loose.

He slammed his fist into the orc's stomach, followed by a brutal kick to the groin. Harruq rammed his elbows into the orc's face, baring his teeth in a feral grin as he felt cartilage crunch. Staggering back, the orc dropped one of his swords and clutched his face.

"His sword," Qurrah shouted loud as he could. "Take it, brother!"

Harruq obeyed without thought. He dropped to his knees, grabbed the sword, and rolled forward. Steel smacked where he had been. Now on his back, Harruq tossed the sword in front of himself, clutching the hilt with both hands. The orc smashed his own blade downward, and as they connected, Harruq did not feel fear or the strain of his muscles. He felt exhilarated. Even though the orc pressed with all his strength, he could not force the kill.

At last, Harruq forced him back, and in the brief opening he spun his sword around and buried half the blade into the orc's gut. The orc gasped something unintelligible, dropped his other sword, and fell limp. Harruq stared at the body, his hands shaking from the excitement and his breath thunderous in his ears. A hand touched his shoulder. He recoiled as if struck.

"Well done," Qurrah said, his eyes locked on the corpse. Harruq recognized that look. His brother had seen something he wanted, and he would have it. "A strong life and a fresh death."

"The battle?" Harruq asked. Even as they stood there, he watched several orcs go running past, howling murder.

"We will partake in our own way," Qurrah said, kneeling beside the orc. The savage clutched his stomach, his hands the only thing holding in his innards. Qurrah's thin, ashen face curled into a sneer. Harruq turned away. Perhaps his brother would think him weak, but he would not watch. He heard a sudden shriek of pain that morphed into a long, drawn-out moan. As the last of the air left the orc's lungs, Harruq turned around, startled by the sight.

"Beauty in all things," Qurrah said, purple light dancing across his face. "Especially those things that are controlled."

An orb floated above his open palm, seemingly made of thick, violet smoke. Within its center, a face shifted, its sunken eyes glaring. When it opened its mouth, no sound came forth, just a soft puff of ash.

"A soul seeking release," Qurrah said. "How destructive, I wonder?"

"Get rid of it," Harruq said as he picked up the other sword the orc had dropped.

"You disagree?" Qurrah asked, his delight vanishing into a sudden frown.

"No," Harruq said. He thought to explain and then just shrugged. "It makes me uneasy," he said instead. "But do as you wish."

The frailer brother approached the end of the alley where the sound of combat was strongest. His steps faltered only once. When Harruq moved to catch him, Qurrah glared and leaned against the side of a house. When a luckless orc rushed too close to the exit, Qurrah hurled the orb. Its explosion conjured shadows and shifting mists of violets and purples. The orc collapsed, white smoke rising softly from his tongue. In the sudden blinding light, Qurrah laughed.

"Never," he said, "could I have imagined it so beautiful."

An hour before dawn, the city's soldiers cornered and killed the last of the orcs. The Tun brothers were not there to watch, for they had snuck back to the outer wall at Qurrah's insistence.

"I know his plans," Qurrah whispered as they stared across the open grass and the arrow-pierced orc bodies that covered it. "He is familiar to me, though I know him not."

"He isn't your former master, is he?" Harruq asked as he adjusted his newly acquired swords. He had taken a belt and some sheaths from one of the dead bodies, but he was having a devil of a time getting them to fit correctly.

"No," Qurrah said. "He is dead. I killed him. Whoever this is, he is someone else. Someone stronger."

He pointed into the darkness.

"There," he said. "He returns."

Robed in black, the figure approached unseen by the guards. He lifted his hands, which shone a pallid white in the fading moonlight. So very slowly their color faded, from white, to gray, to nothing, a darkness surrounding and hiding them.

"What's going on?" Harruq asked. He pulled one of his swords out from its sheath, pleased by the feeling of confidence it gave him. Qurrah said not a word. His eyes were far away, and his lips moved but produced no sound.

"Qurrah?" Harruq asked again. "Qurrah!"

He struck his brother on the arm. Qurrah jolted as if suddenly waking.

"The dead," Qurrah said. "They rise."

Sure enough, the arrow-ridden bodies stirred. As if of one mind, they rose together, ignoring any injuries upon them. Some hobbled on broken legs while others shambled with twisted and mangled arms. The brothers watched as hundreds more lumbered through the still-broken southern gate. A few belated alarms cried out from the exhausted guards, but they were too few and too late. Unencumbered, the horde of dead marched out to where the necromancer extended his arms to embrace them.

Harruq and Qurrah watched until the sun rose in the east and all trace of the necromancer vanished.

"What is it he wanted?" Harruq asked, breaking their long silence.

"More dead for his army," Qurrah surmised.

"No," Harruq said. "With you."

Qurrah nodded, knowing he disrespected his brother to think he might not have noticed.

"He wanted my name," Qurrah said. "I did not give it. I have served a master once. I will not do so again."

Harruq frowned but said no more. Together they climbed down from the wall and returned home.

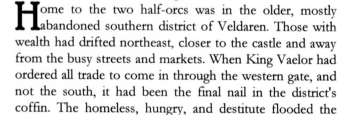

Home to the two half-orcs was in the older, mostly abandoned southern district of Veldaren. Those with wealth had drifted northeast, closer to the castle and away from the busy streets and markets. When King Vaelor had ordered all trade to come in through the western gate, and not the south, it had been the final nail in the district's coffin. The homeless, hungry, and destitute flooded the rows of abandoned buildings, clawing them away from their legal owners with their very presence, or sometimes their murders.

Harruq and Qurrah played that game well. They had grown up on the streets of Veldaren and fought for every scrap of food they'd eaten. They had punched and kicked for every soft, dry bed. Then, one day, they finally killed.

"A fine home is any home that's yours," Harruq said as he forced back a couple planks sealing a window. "Ain't that right, Qurrah?"

"Whatever you say."

Once the window was unblocked, the two climbed in. They lived in what had once been a large shed. The door was still boarded shut, but the window, well...

For two such as they, windows worked as well as doors.

They sat diagonally of each other so they had room to stretch their legs. Harruq unhooked his belt and placed his swords in a corner, brushing their hilts against his fingertips.

"I want to learn how to use them," he said. "Think anyone will teach me?"

Qurrah laughed. "You'll find plenty who'll teach you how to die by one," he said. "I'm not sure about the other way around."

Harruq shrugged. His mind kept replaying the fight with the orc. Untrained and unprepared, he had still won. What could he accomplish with training? How many might fear him if he had skill to match his strength and steel to match his anger?

"I know of a way," Qurrah said, pulling at one of many loose strands of his robes. "A way for you to practice. You saw what I did with that dead body."

Harruq nodded, disturbed by the hungry look in Qurrah's eyes.

"I did," he said, "and it scared the abyss out of me."

Qurrah dismissed this with a wave of his hand. "With exposure comes understanding. I am always in control, so don't fear what I do. But I must learn, Harruq. I have no school, no teacher, nothing but scattered memories of my wretched master when I was nine. Nevertheless, death... death has a way of teaching us things. I can sense its power so clearly in its presence. I need it. You must give it to me."

Harruq crossed his arms and stared into the corner.

"People die every day here," he said. "Shall I find their bodies and bring them to you?"

"For now," Qurrah said. "Yes. If the death is fresh, the power should still linger."

Harruq reached out, grabbed his brother's wrist, and clasped his hands in his.

"I won't like it," he said. "But I'll do it for you."

"We are better than them," Qurrah said, standing so he could look through the cracks of the boards across the broken door. "Stronger. Life is for those who take it. I need you to understand this, brother. Together, we can become something great."

"Like what?" Harruq asked. "What can we become?"

Qurrah's eyes twinkled, but he said not a word.

Guard captain Antonil marched through the street, leading fifty of his men marching in perfect union. His face was a portrait of stoic calm, but it was all a lie. His heart was troubled and he had not a soul to tell why. He held a proclamation of King Vaelor to the entire nation of Neldar. He had argued as best he could, but his words meant little. When Antonil asked that someone else deliver the proclamation, a frown had crossed the king's smooth face and he had slammed his lotioned hand against a table.

"It will mean more coming from you!" the king had shouted. "They will know the seriousness of my order. I will not be flooded with spies, treated like a mere peasant, and then insulted by such blatant snubbing of my humble call for aid. Let them know I am king, my dear Antonil. Make sure they know."

Antonil halted at the center of Veldaren where the four main roads of the city interconnected and a large marble fountain towered over all. Not bothering to call for silence or attention, he unrolled the scroll and shouted its edict. Because of his rank, the troops in attendance, and the overall respect given to the man who had engineered the city's successful defense only days before, he was quickly given a respectful silence.

"By order of the King, all elves are to be removed from Neldar lands. They shall not travel within our cities, live in our settlements, or trade with our people. They are banned in all possible sense of the word. They have abandoned us, so let us abandon them. These are the words of your King, Edwin Vaelor, and may they never be forgotten."

Antonil closed the scroll and then nodded for his soldiers to return to their post. Holding in a curse, he headed to the royal stables. He needed to speak with Dieredon and personally break the terrible news.

Qurrah smirked as the guard captain hurried away.

"Elves banned," he said to his brother. "Amusing, though unnecessary. Only handfuls live within these walls, and they are just diplomats and messengers. Our king is a spiteful, paranoid one."

"Not my king," Harruq muttered loud as he dared. He meant to say more but stopped as another man neared the fountain. He was large, well-muscled, and scratching at a long beard that stretched down to his belt. In a massive voice, he shouted to the mulling throngs.

"The royal guard is in need of able-bodied men to help rebuild the walls of the city," he shouted. "The work will be hard, but we offer a threepence of copper a day. Come to the castle and ask for Alvrik."

He repeated the message three more times and then wandered back north.

"A threepence," Harruq said. "We could eat well for weeks."

"The king must be desperate for workers," Qurrah said. He raised an eyebrow at his brother. "I take it you're interested?"

"I'm strong enough for whatever they want from me," Harruq insisted.

"We have no need for money." Qurrah reminded him. "We take what we need. We always have."

"My days are spent in boredom and you know it," Harruq said. "How long will they offer that much coin?"

Qurrah popped his neck, wincing as he did. "So be it," he conceded. "Take the work…if they'll take you."

This put a bit of a damper on Harruq's enthusiasm.

"Course they will," he muttered, his frown betraying the confidence in his voice. "Why wouldn't they?"

"**A**lvrik," Harruq muttered as he approached the giant double doors leading into the castle, which were flanked on each side by two soldiers. "Avrik? Alrik? Avlerik? How the bloody abyss did he say his name?"

He stopped when he realized the soldiers were staring at him with none-too-happy looks on their faces.

"Oh, hello," he said, doing his best to smile. "I was looking for, er, Alvrik. He was just in the center of town, and…"

"Does the orcie want some money?" one of the guards asked. He jabbed his elbow into the soldier next to him as both laughed in Harruq's face.

"Just want some work," he grumbled, his deep voice almost impossible to understand.

"Head around back," one told him. "Alvrik will be waiting."

"That'd be west," said the same rude guard. "You know which way west is, right?"

Harruq's hands opened and closed as he imagined his swords within them, ready to butcher for blood while the soldier proceeded to say the word 'west' as long and drawn out as possible.

"Thanks," he mumbled and hurried off.

Accompanied by a young man scribbling on a sheet of parchment, Alvrik sat at a small table in front of a group of people waiting in line to address him. Harruq slipped into the back and tried to calm down. Never before had he done anything like this. He had stolen food, fled from guards, lived in poverty, and kept to himself. For he and his brother, that was life. What the abyss was he doing asking for work?

A swelling of nerves in his gut almost forced him to leave. Several men in front of him turned away, dejected or angry. He didn't hear the reasons why and didn't want to know. The idea of so much money, more than enough to buy warm food and clean drink, kept him there. At last it was his turn, and he approached the table where Alvrik sat chewing on a piece of bone long since void of meat.

"You," he said before Harruq could mutter a word. "You don't look like all the others."

"I'm not like the others."

"That so?" Alvrik's face hadn't changed in the slightest. "Tell me why."

"Stronger," he said. "Tougher. Whatever work you got two men doing, I can do alone. Whatever hours you got them working, I can do double."

"A large boast," Alvrik said. He took the bone out of his mouth and pointed at Harruq's ears. "You got orc blood in you."

"I do."

"Will that be a problem?" Alvrik asked.

"Up to all the others you hire," Harruq said. "But I'll be fine. I don't start much, but I always finish."

Alvrik laughed. He nudged the man next to him, who grabbed the quill.

"Give me your name," he asked, dabbing the tip into the ink.

"Harruq," he said. "Harruq Tun."

"Well, Harruq," Alvrik said, slowly nodding his head. "I'll see you right here at sunrise tomorrow. Got that?"

Harruq grinned ear to ear, even his nervousness unable to diminish his excitement.

"I'll be here before the rooster knows it's dawn."

A sharp pain in his gut dragged Harruq from his dreams. He lifted open a single eye and glared at the blurry image of his brother.

"The sun is almost up," Qurrah said, kicking him again. "You need to be as well."

"What are you...awww, damn it."

He sat up straight and shook his head, trying to clear the fuzz that clogged the vast empty space between his ears. Qurrah helped by offering a third kick, this one right to the kidney. Harruq gasped and staggered to his feet. He was outside their little home in seconds, urinating on the grass.

"Hadn't pissed yet," Harruq shouted to his brother. "You could be a bit kinder, you know."

"At least you're awake," Qurrah said back. "Now get to the castle. I may not approve, and I still don't trust them, but for once we might have something worthwhile to eat. I won't let a simple thing like sleep keep us from it."

2

Months later, Harruq awoke at the dawn, jerking upward and uttering a sharp gasp. A constant cry of danger rang in his ears. A quick survey showed he slept alone in their small shed, his brother missing.

"Qurrah?" he dared ask.

"Outside," came Qurrah's muffled reply.

Harruq stretched, pushed away a plank of wood from the window, and climbed out. The sun was halfway visible, the standard noises of the city only in their infancy. Leaning against the shed, his eyes staring off toward the sunrise, waited Qurrah.

"What are you doing out here?" Harruq asked.

"Did you sense it?" Qurrah asked.

"Sense what?"

The smaller half-orc shook his head.

"If you must ask then you did not, at least not directly, though I did hear you startle awake. Perhaps a fleeting glimpse of it…"

"Qurrah," Harruq said, crossing his arms and frowning at him. "What is this about? Tell me."

"Remember the necromancer we witnessed at the siege?" Qurrah asked. "It is him. He has haunted my dreams lately, and today he whispered the name of a place I have already researched for my own purposes. I think we are being guided, though I dare not pretend to know why."

Harruq shifted, the dark expression on his brother's face making him uncomfortable.

"What's the place?" he asked.

"It is where our mother came from," Qurrah said. "A town called Woodhaven. Well, two towns really, Celed and Singhelm. They have since grown together and merged. It is an interesting place, Harruq, where elves and men live together, each in their respective parts of the city. Their tolerance of other races is, obviously, a necessity. I have thought to take us there."

"Why do we need to leave?"

"Your work is almost done," Qurrah said. "The walls are repaired, and half the men who worked with you have already been cut loose. I, however, have much to learn but cannot do so here because of prying eyes and attentive ears. I need privacy. I need silence."

"What for?" Harruq asked.

"No," Qurrah said. "Don't ask when you full well know the answer."

At this Harruq nodded. Yes, he did know. Over the past few months, he had killed seven men and carried their bodies to his brother.

"I still have at least a week," Harruq said. "Give me until then, alright? We could use the money."

"I have saved much of what you earned," Qurrah said. "We will be able to eat, not well, but enough to live."

"If you say so," Harruq said. "Good luck with your, uh, studies. I have a wall to finish building."

"Stay safe," Qurrah said, offering a small wave as his brother trudged north. When he was gone, the smaller half-orc slipped back into the shed, removed a false floorboard, and grasped a small pouch containing various herbs, bones, and knives. Reaching back in again, he took out an object wrapped in sackcloth and soaked in blood. A knife in hand, he opened the pouch and closed his eyes. His mind attuned, he carved into the remains of a man's heart.

On his way back home, the threepence jingling in his hand, Harruq spotted a patrol of guards approaching. He glanced to the right, where the small alley led back to their shed. If he hurried, he might be able to make it before they noticed...

He was halfway down the alley when he heard a voice call out.

"Hey!"

Harruq kept going. He was used to harassment and verbal abuse from the guards. Once out of sight, though, he was usually out of mind. He relied on that as he turned a corner into the small space around their shed. Qurrah, who had been resting on the shallow grass, hurried to his feet at Harruq's approach.

"What is the matter?" he asked.

"Nothing, but you might want to hide in there. Quick!"

"I will do no such thing," Qurrah said.

"I said hey!" shouted the same man. Harruq stepped in front of Qurrah and then turned, staring down a group of five heavily armored guards. Swords and clubs hung from their belts, though a fifth carried a weapon neither of them had ever seen before. It was a wooden stick with a bulbous gem on one end.

"You stop when asked or pay the price," said one of the guards.

"If he can even understand us," said another.

"We understand perfectly," Qurrah said, stepping to one side. "What has my brother done to warrant your attention?"

"We're on a quest," said the man wielding the strange weapon. He had a stubbly beard and a hooked nose with a thick scar along the top. "A great quest from the king, you could say. We're to rid scum from the city, elven scum. You know what I think? I think elves can look like anything. They're devious little pricks like that, and you two seem rather ugly and devious, don't you all agree?"

The other guards laughed and shouted in agreement. They had spread out, flanking the half-orcs on all sides. The leader stepped forward and gestured with his weapon.

"You know what this is? This detects elves, and every elf I find I get to politely escort out of the city. Oh, and their possessions, well, obviously they were stolen. That coin you got there, you might as well hand it over before I take it."

Qurrah glared while Harruq clutched the coins tighter and fought down his anger. He glanced back to the shed, cursing his idiocy for not retrieving his weapons while he had the chance.

"The coin," demanded a guard to their right. "Hand it over."

"No," Harruq said.

The leader rammed his fist into the half-orc's face. Harruq staggered but held his ground. Blood ran down his face, and he spat some away from his mouth. He waited for another punch, but nothing came. The man was staring in total disbelief at the weapon he held. As he had stepped closer to punch, the gem at the end had shimmered a soft green.

"Of all the dumb luck," he said, a grin spreading across his face. "We got some real elves here!"

They drew their swords. Harruq held an arm defensively in front of Qurrah, his eyes darting in all directions. Slowly, the leader extended the stick, poking it against Harruq's chest. The soft glow turned into a brilliant flare of emerald.

"Elves," the man said. "No doubt about it."

He laughed to the others and then punched Harruq in the gut. As the half-orc doubled over, the guard grabbed his hair and tugged.

"Got to be a disguise," he said. Another guard used the hilt of his sword to strike Harruq's back. The blow blasted the air out of his lungs. The leader of the guards tugged all along Harruq's face, pulling hair and scratching skin.

"I'll be," he said. "It is real. No illusion and no disguise. You two cretins have god-damned elf blood in you."

"You jest," Qurrah said, hanging back and showing no sign of aggression. The soldiers clearly thought Harruq the more dangerous of the two, and he was more than willing to let them continue thinking that.

"No jest," the guard said. "You two are leaving this city, now."

"My things," Harruq said, his voice coming out as a weak croak.

"I don't see anything," said the guard, scooping down and retrieving the scattered coins Harruq had dropped.

"In the shed," Qurrah said.

"That where you two live?"

"Yes."

"Fine," the leader said. "Go and get whatever the abyss you can carry."

Harruq climbed into the shed, throwing Qurrah a worried look before he did. When he came out holding his sheathed swords to his chest, the guards tensed, readying their weapons.

"Drop those right now," they ordered him. Harruq clutched them tight, and the look on his face was clear. He would fight, and die, before he gave them up. The lead guard, already having their coin as well as the bonus of having found elves in hiding, was willing to let it slide.

"You draw them, even fiddle with them in their sheaths, you die, that clear?" he told the half-orc. Harruq nodded, again saying nothing.

"Calm yourself," Qurrah whispered to his brother as the two marched in front of the guards toward the main streets.

"Trying," Harruq whispered back.

They marched at sword point. Onlookers cackled as they passed, figuring the two were thieves or vagrants caught brawling. Their orcish features lent them no kindness, and a few children even threw rocks until the guards shooed them away. The whole while Harruq burned with shame and rage.

They reached the western gate, which remained open during the day. Without ceremony, they were kicked through, both falling to the dirt and scraping their knees.

"Get going," one said. "See if somewhere else will take your mutt ass."

It was not just adrenaline that caused Harruq's hands to shake, but Qurrah put his hand on his wrist and begged him to calm.

"Never forget this shame," he said. "Let it burn in you. Let it be a reminder of what I have always said. We are better, superior. Never feel guilt at what we do to them, for you see what they would do to us."

Harruq stood, brushed some dirt from his pants, and then offered Qurrah a hand. Together they trudged west, without food, water, or blankets. The guards watched them go, smirking all the while.

That night Harruq collected a bunch of sticks and twigs, which Qurrah lit with a clap of his hands. The two huddled over the fire, each lost in their thoughts. Harruq broke the silence first.

"So where will we go?" he asked.

"Where else is there?" Qurrah said. "Perhaps we were meant to go to Woodhaven. The journey will not be long, perhaps a week or two at most. There are enough animals about for me to kill, so do not worry about food. As for water, there are many small streams, and we can beg from the occasional farms we pass. We were to leave anyway, now we do so sooner."

"Sooner?" Harruq said. "We paraded through the city like criminals and were tossed out with swords at our backs. If we were to leave, I wanted to leave on our own terms, not like that."

He swore a few times, getting progressively more colorful as he went.

"Two minutes alone with that guard," he muttered. "I'd have him drinking through a brand new hole in his neck."

"How skilled are you with those?" Qurrah asked, gesturing at the swords in the grass next to Harruq. Even though they lived in such cramped quarters, Qurrah still knew very little of Harruq's life other than what he did at his request.

"I've watched the guards training new men," Harruq said, drawing a blade and holding it with one hand. "And I've been practicing every night after you're in bed and no one is around to watch and get curious. Near the castle they have these stumps for smacking with your sword. Not sure what for, but it helps them, and it seemed to help me. I snuck over there plenty of times. No one guards a big, beaten log."

"But you have yet to face men in combat," Qurrah said. "Do not be overzealous about your skills. Confident, perhaps, but not foolish. Don't die on me, brother, for I need you more than ever."

"Yeah, I know," Harruq said, growing quiet. The subject of Qurrah's experiments always made him uneasy.

"This time there will be a slight difference," Qurrah said.

"What's that?"

The half-orc shook his head.

"Not now. Another time I will explain."

The two grew quiet, and they stared at the fire as the time passed. At last, when Harruq was sure Qurrah would not bring up the subject, he spoke.

"About the guards," he said. "You think they're telling the truth?"

Qurrah glanced up.

"About the elven blood in us?"

"Yeah."

Qurrah chuckled, but it was mirthless.

"I do, and it does not surprise me as much as it should. I'm not sure who would mate with our mother, but some elf man did. We are smarter than most realize, you know that. Our features are sharper, and we only resemble the orcs that attacked Veldaren. It is a part of us. Unwanted, perhaps, but I shall not cower and hide a part of who I am."

"Just strange, is all," Harruq said.

"Life is strange."

They both lay down to rest, a new life awaiting them in Woodhaven.

3

In silence, Harruq Tun stared at the body. Seven, he guessed. No older than seven. He didn't know the boy's name or why he had wandered into the forest. The bloodied corpse was sprawled across the knotted roots of a tree, its innards spilled through a massive gash from shoulder to waist. The eyes remained open, their young innocence spoiled by a lingering look of horror.

You're an orc, aren't you?

Harruq snarled and shook his head. He shouldn't have spoken to him. Shouldn't have let him ask questions. The last of his adrenaline faded as images of the child's quivering lips and trembling hands haunted his vision.

"Half," Harruq whispered as he wiped blood from his swords onto the grass. "Only half."

The kill had been quick, just a single cut through the shoulder blade, the heart, and then the lung. No suffering, little pain. It was all he could offer.

"He's dead, Qurrah," the half-orc shouted. His deep voice, like a bear's growl, seemed right at home in the forest. "Come on over."

Qurrah approached through the trees, clutching a worn bag in his long fingers. His brown eyes glanced over the dead boy. He nodded in approval.

"Well done," Qurrah said.

"Killing kids is hardly worth a well done."

Qurrah frowned as he glanced from his prize to his brother, who sat against a tree, arms on his knees. "Take pride in all you do," Qurrah said. "Only then will you improve."

Harruq shrugged. "You need me?"

The smaller half-orc opened the bag he carried. Inside were ashes, roots, herbs, and a sharpened knife: all Qurrah needed to work his art.

"No. You may go."

Harruq rose, glanced at the body, and then departed.

"What are they looking at?" Harruq later asked as the two brothers walked down the winding streets of Woodhaven.

"Let us see," said Qurrah.

Harruq muscled his way past two men, his brother following in his wake. They found a proclamation nailed to a post.

"What's it say?" Harruq asked.

"All children are to be kept outside the boundary of the forest," Qurrah said, his eyes narrowing. "Six have been killed by the…"

Qurrah laughed, a hideous sound.

"By the what?" Harruq asked.

"The Forest Butcher," said an aged woman next to him, her voice creaking as if she had tiny pebbles lodged in her throat. She glanced back to the worn brown paper. "Hope they find him. Been a long time since we had an execution, but whoever that sick bastard is deserves a gruesome one."

"Such hatred in a meager body," Qurrah said, and his smile earned him a sneer.

"Come on, Qurrah. I'm getting hungry," Harruq said as he trudged off, his hands at his sides grabbing the air where his swords no longer were.

The two brothers lived in the poorest part of town, sheltered in an old building long abandoned. When they had first arrived, several homeless men claimed it as their own. Harruq had slit their throats when they slept and then Qurrah worked his art. The few vagabonds left in the city quickly learned to avoid the worn building marked by holes in its roof and long shadows that lingered no matter where the sun shone.

Harruq shoved open the door and then halted as he breathed in the stuffy air.

"Nothing like home, eh?" he said.

"Move, before the meat spoils," Qurrah said.

The big half-orc stepped out of the way. Qurrah came through, carrying a slab of meat in his hands. He weaved across the missing planks in the floor and sat next to a small circle of stones. Above him was a hole in the ceiling for the smoke to escape.

"Since when has spoiling meat stopped me from eating it?" Harruq asked.

Qurrah laughed. "Which explains so much."

Murmuring a few words, he smashed his hands together. Fire burst to life in the center of the stones. Harruq grabbed a small pot and brought it to the fire, but Qurrah stopped him.

"There is no need," he said.

"How come?" Harruq asked.

Qurrah narrowed his eyes and stared at the meat in his hands.

"I have something I wish to try."

The bigger half-orc stepped back, willing to watch his brother work. While Harruq was skilled in swords and had all the muscle, Qurrah possessed far more interesting talents.

Qurrah mumbled words, sick and spidery. The bones in the slab of meat snapped erect as if pulled by invisible strings. He kept whispering, his eyes wide. The meat floated from his hands and then lowered into the fire. Qurrah twirled his finger, and the slab turned as if on a spit.

"We're eating fancy tonight," Harruq said, tossing the pot back to its corner. His stomach growled as the aroma of cooked meat filled his nostrils.

"Glad you approve," Qurrah said.

They ate in silence until only bones remained, which Qurrah then tucked away in a pouch. Harruq relaxed and enjoyed the heat while his brother tightened his robe and leaned toward the fire.

"Things are more dangerous now, aren't they?" Harruq asked after a pause.

Qurrah nodded, his thoughts distant. "They're ready for us. Many elves will be lurking inside the woods as they hunt for the Forest Butcher." Again Qurrah chuckled at the name his brother had earned.

"Will we stop for a while?" Harruq asked.

The smaller half-orc shook his head. "Of course not. I must keep learning, increasing my strength. We will resume, just this time amid the darkness."

Harruq nodded, obviously uneasy. "Hey brother?"

"Yes Harruq?"

"Are you sure what we're doing isn't wrong?" He twiddled his fingers, suddenly embarrassed. "I mean… they're children."

Qurrah sighed. He had sensed apprehension in his brother before, especially when it came to the children. Such nuisances needed to be eradicated.

"If given a choice," Qurrah asked, "would you split a seed or burn a flower? Let the children meet their end before they learn the torment and anguish of their parents. Besides, kill a child and the mother has one less mouth to feed. Kill the mother or father and all the children suffer and starve."

The larger half-orc shrugged. He was not convinced but that mattered little. He would trust his wiser brother as he always had. Qurrah let his eyes drift back to the fire. "Tomorrow night, bring me a body, but don't let yourself be caught. A gruesome execution does not suit my immediate plans."

"Sure," Harruq said. "Whatever you want."

They slept in their pile of hay and cloth. Harruq did not wake until late morning, but Qurrah slept far less. The dream had come again.

34

*W*oodhaven *burned behind him, billowing smoke. The sun was gone, and no stars penetrated the blanket of rainless clouds that loomed above. Far away, a wolf howled.*

Come to me, *said a voice. Qurrah looked to the distance. He could see a man cloaked in black standing upon a hill. Red eyes burned through the blackness within his hood. The feeling of absolute power then was greater than Qurrah had ever felt, greater than even the master of his youth.*

Why should I follow? *Qurrah heard himself ask. Hands stretched to the heavens, the cloaked man laughed. His power surged with the laughter, obliterating Qurrah's ability to stand.*

Because I am eternal, *said the figure.* I sire war. I sow bloodshed. I create my dead, and the dead follow.

What must I do? *Qurrah asked.*

You know the words.

As the dream began to shatter, the words did indeed come to his mind. He could have everything he desired, but to obtain it he must give all he had.

My life for you.

Those were the words.

*T*he following night, Harruq slipped out into the street. Lamps were lit here and there, casting shadows across the road. Harruq stayed far from Celed, the elven side of town, since they sent all their children to be raised in Nellassar, deep in the heart of the Erze forest. It was the human children, especially the poor and the destitute, that Harruq sought. Of course, none would be out playing, not with so many dead and missing. He would need to take different measures.

Not far from their home, a ratty building operated throughout the night. It was Maggie's Place, half tavern and half orphanage. Maggie enjoyed the free labor and the ability to rant and slap her orphan workers without fear of reprisal while still maintaining the image of a heart of gold to her regulars. The tavern filled the first floor, while the orphanage and a few modest rooms for rent composed the second.

Harruq stepped into the alley beside the tavern and looked up. A window. Perfect. As he searched for a way to scale the wall, he saw a drunken man watching him.

"Get lost," Harruq growled. The man obliged, taking his bottle of ale and running. That taken care of, the half-orc went around back where he found a few worn and uneven crates. He lifted one and approved of its strength after a simple test. Satisfied, he went back around and placed it against the wall. He was about to go back for a second when torchlight flooded the alley.

"Move and you'll find an arrow in your throat," said a voice.

"Pincushion him anyway," urged another.

Harruq held a hand before his eyes, cursing his awful luck. He saw two figures, night patrolmen, and both human. One had a readied bow aimed at his neck.

"I haven't done anything wrong," Harruq said.

"Sure you haven't," one of the patrolmen said. "Then what's with the crate?"

The half-orc's mind groped for a reason. "Um, well, I needed to piss, so I came out here."

"So you needed that to go behind?" asked the other. Harruq nodded. "Bullshit. Put your hands up. I see those sword hilts."

Harruq mumbled another curse, his pulse racing. It wouldn't take long to down the closer soldier, provided the archer wasn't too good a shot. Even then, he risked at least two arrows sticking in his flesh. Unsure of what to do, he played dumb and let the first soldier approach.

"Careful, he's a biggie," the bowman said.

"Nothing I can't handle," said the other before smashing the butt of his sword into Harruq's face. Rage surged through the half-orc's veins, his orcish side screaming for blood. He fought it down even as a mailed fist smashed against his spine. Harruq collapsed to his knees, choking down a furious roar.

"Goes down easy, I say," the guard said to the bowman. "How much you want to bet this guy is the sick bastard killing the kids?"

"How much you wanna bet we can hang him even if he isn't?" the other asked.

Both guards laughed, and the sickness in Harruq's gut grew. A boot kicked his stomach, and he knew his patience was near its end. Visions of ripping out entrails filled his mind, and all his willpower kept him crouched there. A kick to the face forced him over, and he reached for the impact point along his cheek. A sword hilt quickly found his exposed chest. Rolling over only shifted the next few blows to his back. When the heel of a boot crushed down on his kidney, Harruq felt ready to slaughter, no longer caring if he was caught or killed. He would make them both pay.

The tip of a sword pressed against the side of his neck, drawing blood from the slightest pressure.

"He looks mad," said the guard. "Died fighting us, don't that sound right?"

Every muscle in Harruq's body tensed, knowing his moment to act would need to be perfect. Before he could, a feminine voice shouted down the alley, startling all three.

"Both of you, stop that this instant!"

Through blurred vision, Harruq saw a woman with auburn hair standing at the edge of the alley. The patrolmen also turned to look, their weapons still in hand.

"Who the abyss…oh, go on back to your forest, Aurelia. Nothing to see here."

The woman pointed to the bleeding half-orc.

"I see plenty."

"Just cleaning up some filth." The bowman shifted his bow onto his shoulder. "Now move along."

"I don't see any filth. Some blood and dirt, maybe, but no filth."

Harruq closed his eyes and listened as he tried to slow his pulse. He had no clue who this Aurelia was, but if she wanted to intervene he was glad to let her.

"This does not concern you, elf," said one of the guards.

Harruq coughed at this. The woman saving him was an elf? Had the world turned upside down?

"Oh really?" Aurelia said. "How sad."

"We said go, now, or else."

"Or else what?"

The sword point left Harruq's neck, and he assumed the guard made a threatening gesture. The next few seconds were a jumble. Sounds of surprised yells and sizzling fire filled the alleyway. The half-orc lifted his head, gasping at what he saw. One of the night patrol stood knee deep in dried mud. The other was hanging upside down from a flaming whip that failed to burn him.

"Get on up, orc," Aurelia said. "Or half-orc, whatever you are. I can only keep them like this for a little while."

Both men glared at Harruq as he stood, but while their mouths moved and their chests heaved neither produced a sound. The half-orc looked to the woman shrouded in the shadows cast by the fallen torch of the patrolmen.

"I said move along," she said. "I need to give these men a talking to."

"I'm going," Harruq grumbled before staggering down the alley. He did not attempt either stealth or silence. Seething, he limped back to Qurrah and their home. Neither said a word as he discarded his armor, tossed his swords into a corner, and crashed onto their bed of straw. For a long moment, only the sound of Harruq's heavy breathing filled the room.

"I assume things didn't go well?" Qurrah finally asked. Harruq didn't bother to answer.

◄╪►

*T*he swarming sensation of power enveloped him. Beneath angry clouds, the man with red eyes beckoned.

I am waiting, *he said.* All the power of Dezrel is waiting.

What must I do? *Qurrah asked as he crept up the hill toward the dark man as if approaching a god.*

You know the words.

Can I trust you?

The red eyes flared in laughter. Can you trust anyone?

Qurrah crawled faster, knowing the dream was ending. But it couldn't end. He had to know. He had to decide.

Say them. Say them and live.

My life for you, *Qurrah shouted as the world crystallized. A red line slashed across his mind, and as the dream shattered into shards the words of the dark man ripped through him.*

Then come reap the rewards.

Qurrah lurched awake, gasping for air. His throat ached, and he could feel the tiniest trickle of blood down his trachea. The night was still deep and the town quiet. Beside him, Harruq snored loud enough to wake the drunkest of men. Far away, a wolf howl beckoned.

"Sleep well," Qurrah said, leaving the town.

His doubt faded with each step. All was identical to his dreams. A mile from town, he saw the hill, a smoldering fire atop it to guide his way. Waiting there was the dark man, his red eyes shining down on him as he approached.

"Say the words," the man in the black robe ordered. His voice was quiet but deep, a mixture of hate and malice compressed into audible form.

"How can I make such a promise to one whose name I don't know?" Qurrah asked. In answer, the man in black stood. His eyes flared and his arms spread wide. All his power rolled forth, and on trembling knees the half-orc looked upon a man more ancient than the forests, more powerful than the fury of nature, and more death than life.

"My life for you," he gasped as a fresh wave of terror crawled over him.

"I would have it no other way," the man in black said. "Now tell me your name."

"I am Qurrah Tun."

"And I am Velixar. Rise, Qurrah, and join me by the fire. Ever since I felt your presence back at Veldaren, I have yearned to speak with you."

The half-orc took his seat opposite the man. He stared at Velixar, hardly believing what he saw. His face was smooth, his lips small, and his sunken eyes glowing a deep crimson. His features, however, kept changing. Every time Qurrah blinked the man's face reassembled in some minutely different way. No matter how high or low his nose, or how wide or narrow his forehead, those burning eyes remained.

"What are you?" Qurrah asked.

Velixar laughed.

"How much do you know of the gods of this world, Qurrah Tun?"

Qurrah shrugged. "I know their names and little else. Karak is death, Ashhur is life, and Celestia everything else, if the ramblings of priests and elves is to be believed."

Velixar nodded, the fire in his eyes growing. "This world is young, Qurrah, and Karak and Ashhur are young gods. Only five-hundred years ago they came and gave life to man." Those eyes twinkled. "I was one of the first they made."

The half-orc pulled his ragged robe tighter about him as he stared into the fire. "How is that possible?" he asked. A soft wind blew, making the fire dance, and in the flickering flames Velixar smiled.

"I was the favorite of Karak, my dear orcish friend. He gave me life when other men would have long turned to dust. When he was defeated, and his servants were cast into the abyss, I alone escaped punishment."

"I am not orcish," Qurrah said, harsher than he meant.

Velixar raised his hand in a small gesture of apology. "Orcish blood is in your veins, but perhaps I am mistaken. What are you then?"

"I am a half-orc," Qurrah said. His shoulders hunched, and his head lowered as a reluctant bit of shame stung his words. "The blood of both elves and orcs fills my veins."

He expected to be scoffed, mocked, or banished. Instead, Velixar laughed.

"Such blasphemy against the elven goddess," he said. "Appropriate, so appropriate. You have sworn your life to me, half-orc. You should learn what you stand to gain."

The cloaked man reached across the fire. His fingers brushed Qurrah's pale face. Sudden, awful pain pierced his skull. Visions flowed through those fingers, dominant and brutal.

Qurrah marched through a burning city commanding a legion of walking dead. Screams of men and women sang a constant chorus, and in the distance, a castle crumbled to stone and dust. A demonic chant filled his ears, two words repeated again and again. It was a warcry against all life.

"For Qurrah! For Qurrah!"

As the vision faded, one last sight burned into Qurrah's mind: it was he, dressed in deep robes of black, his eyes glowing a bloody crimson.

That was Veldaren," Qurrah said as Velixar's fingers pulled back. He felt awe and fear at the sight of the magnificent city ablaze.

"I want all of Neldar to burn," Velixar said, his deep voice rumbling. "Will you aid me?"

Such a great request, a desire for destruction that most would hesitate before. For Qurrah, though, it was a fate he had long expected. It was within his blood, the cursed, the race of the ugly and the destructive. Yet it had been his elvish blood that had him banished. Such foolishness. Such idiocy.

"King Vaelor cowers at the very thought of an elf," Qurrah said. "The rest of the city despises us for the orc within me. I will punish all of their ignorance."

"Tomorrow night, come to me," Velixar said. "I have much to discuss and you have much to learn."

Qurrah stood and bowed before his new master. "I will be here," he said. "And I will be ready."

"Go." Velixar waved his hand, and Qurrah obeyed.

Harruq was still snoring when Qurrah returned to bed. If he had not been so preoccupied, he would have noticed the slight irregularity of the snoring and the exaggerated movements of his brother's chest.

4

Harruq hurried down the road, doing his best to pretend he knew what he was doing. Most of his bruises had already faded, hidden beneath the gray hue of his skin. He drew many glances, however, and he did his best to ignore them. The people of Woodhaven accepted him but still viewed his blood in bad regard. Elves and humans held little love for the orcish kind and had ever since their creation. That distaste suited Harruq just fine. Deep down, Harruq felt he deserved their ire.

He stopped by Maggie's Place, not bothering to go inside. It was early morning and anyone already drinking would hardly be useful. Instead, he stopped the first random passerby that appeared to be a kindly person.

"Do you know of a woman named Aurelia?" he asked, butchering the pronunciation. The passerby, an elderly woman, sneered at him.

"Have fun finding that forest slut," she said before walking on. Harruq shrugged, deciding his ability to pick kindly people wasn't very impressive. He tried again, this time with a tired man trudging down the street.

"Never heard of her," the man said. A few more unsuccessful attempts sent Harruq away from Singhelm and further into Celed. There the reception toward him took a significant turn for the worse. Many refused to meet his eye or acknowledge his question. The half-orc's frustration grew.

"That's it," he muttered to himself. "Just one more and I'm going home. To the abyss with all this." An elf approached. He had long brown hair, walnut eyes, and an elaborate bow slung on his back. The hardened look on his face gave Harruq little hope.

"Do you know of a woman named Aurelia?" he asked anyway.

"Aurelia?" the elf asked. "Why in all of Dezrel would you be looking for her?"

"She, um, I kind of…" The half-orc faltered. "I owe her a favor."

The elf smiled as if trying to appear amused, but it faltered miserably.

"You are looking in the wrong place," he said. "Search the woods just outside town. Call her name a couple times. She'll hear you."

"Thank you," Harruq said, grateful even though his insides churned. He had faced many men in battle, and yet here he was, his heart skipping beats at the thought of meeting this mysterious Aurelia. What was wrong with him?

"You are welcome, half-orc," the elf said before moving on, the bow still hung comfortably on his back. Harruq watched him go, staring longer than he felt he should. He couldn't shake the feeling he was being led into a trap.

"So be it," he said. He would not be afraid of meeting an elf in battle. Grumbling, he stormed off for the forest.

><&><

"Aurelia!"

No answer.

"Aurelia! It's me, from last night! Can you hear me?"

Only the calm, scattered sounds of the forest returned his call.

"Damn elf," Harruq grumbled, crossing his arms and looking all about. "She's probably not here. He just sent me out here to look stupid yelling at trees."

"And what elf would that be?" asked a familiar voice from behind. Harruq whirled, his heart jumping as Aurelia stepped out from behind a tree.

To his eyes, she was even more beautiful in the streaming daylight. Long auburn hair trailed past her shoulders, curled, and ended in several thin braids. Her face and eyes were small, the curve of her bones soft and elegant. She had small lips locked in a frown as she stood cross-armed, as if waiting on him. Her ears, upturned at the peak, were tiny even for her race. She wore a long green dress bound by a golden sash.

"Well? Who sent you here?" she asked. "Was it some mean man trying to toy with you?"

"I'm sorry," Harruq said before resuming his slack-jawed staring. Aurelia uncrossed her arms, those same soft features turning remarkably fierce as she glared at him.

"Stop that. If you don't shut your mouth, I'm turning you into a toad."

He shut his mouth.

"So why are you here?" she asked.

"I was just, um, I never got a chance to thank you." Harruq felt his face flush. This was the most awful thing he had ever done. He'd prefer to face a dragon in unarmed combat. He'd have better odds surviving, too, based on Aurelia's cold, steeled look.

"You came all the way out here to thank me? Hardly sounds like an orcish thing to do."

One would not have thought gray skin could turn so red, but it did.

"Well, I still want to repay you." Harruq held out a small bag containing copper coins. "It's all I have. Please, take it."

Aurelia glanced at the bag. "No," she said.

"But why?"

The elf shook her head. "Your swords. Where are they?"

Harruq glanced at his waist. "They're at my home," he said.

"Are you any good with them?"

The half-orc shrugged. "Better than most. So yeah."

The elf looked him up and down, sending chills roaring along his spine. It seemed so strange that she had saved his life, since at that moment he felt like all she wanted was to see him dead.

"Come tomorrow with swords to spar," she said at last, tucking a few strands of hair behind her ear. "You can train me to wield my staff in melee combat."

"I don't see a staff," Harruq said.

"I don't see any swords either," she shot back.

"Fine. When?"

"Tomorrow," Aurelia said. "Early morning."

Harruq nodded, his whole body fidgeting. Now that he'd found her he wanted nothing more than to escape. He was supposed to thank her and go, not be mocked and ordered around.

"Go on home," Aurelia said. "I'll be waiting for you."

He did as commanded, and that fact disturbed him greatly. Qurrah was awake when he returned.

"Where have you been?" he asked.

"I went out to train," Harruq said.

"Without them?" Qurrah pointed to Harruq's swords stacked in the corner. The larger half-orc shrugged.

"Didn't need them."

Harruq went to the other side of the house and started punching holes in the walls. Qurrah might have inquired further but he was lost in his own secret. The night didn't come soon enough for either of the two brothers.

The air was cold, a sudden chill from the north chasing away the heat of the day. Qurrah wrapped himself best he could as he climbed the hill. He spotted the small fire, and beside it Velixar bathed in its red glow. The fledgling necromancer took his seat across from the man in black.

"Are you ready to listen?" Velixar asked. Qurrah nodded. "Good. The story of this world's gods is not lengthy, nor complicated, but it is a story that you must learn.

"Celestia created the rock, the grass, and the water. Her hand formed the wildlife, and to tend her creation she created elves. The goddess gave them long life and abundant land so quarrels within their race were of the petty sort. Then the brother gods came. Ashhur of Justice, Karak of Order. There are many worlds beyond our own, Qurrah. I have seen fleeting glimpses of them in my dreams. Karak and Ashhur came from one of those worlds, and Celestia welcomed them. To them she gave the grasslands and rolling hills.

"These brother gods did not make their own creation. Instead, they made man, much the same as man existed in their former world. They wanted to make a paradise, one of justice and order. The world they came from was full of chaos, death, and murder. This world, this land of Dezrel, would be different."

Both men shared a soft laugh, Velixar's far bitterer than Qurrah's.

"What caused their failure?" Qurrah asked.

"Karak and Ashhur spoiled their creations. Crops grew bountiful and healthy. A single prayer cured all sickness and disease. Mankind spread across the land with remarkable speed, forming two kingdoms. East of the Rigon River was Neldar, ruled by Karak. To the west was Mordan, governed by Ashhur. However, there was a delta at the end of the river controlled by none. Within were a few small villages with no government, no ruler. Karak brought his troops to establish order. Ashhur was quick to defend it, and in turn, claim it as his own."

"You speak of centuries ago," Qurrah interrupted. "Yet you claim to be one of Karak's first."

"I was his high priest, half-orc," Velixar said, his eyes narrowing. "He blessed me so I would never die of sickness, age, or blade. I have watched the world evolve, and I have watched gods make war. Do not accuse me of having a lying tongue. The truth is always enough, even for those who walk in the darkness."

"Forgive me, master," Qurrah said, bowing. His teeth chattered in the cold.

Velixar waved a hand. The dwindling fire between them swelled to a healthy blaze.

"The two brothers were arrogant to think they could create a paradise with a creature so full of faults as man," Velixar continued. "I saw the battle waged in the small town of Haven, there in the center of the delta. It is an awesome thing to watch gods duel. Ashhur fled before either could strike a killing blow. I summoned our armies, as did the priests of Ashhur. Think now of the many deformed creatures that walk this world. Know they were all mere animals before the gods turned them into soldiers for their war. The elves were vicious in this time, slaying any who dared come near their forests. But some elves did side with Karak, determined to help end the war so the world could heal."

"Did Celestia not interfere?" Qurrah asked.

In the darkness, Qurrah watched as Velixar's face curled into a deep snarl.

"Celestia befriended both brothers, but she took Ashhur to be her lover. She begged each to stop, though neither listened. It was a dark time, Qurrah. All squabbles and wars since are a pittance compared. Ashhur's great city of Mordeina nearly toppled to my hand, but then the priests of Ashhur brought the dead to life to fight against us. Yes, Qurrah, it was the priests of Ashhur, not Karak, who first created the undead. We were beaten back, forced into Veldaren with little hope of survival."

The man in black removed his hood to reveal a long scar. It ran from his left ear, across his throat, and down past the neck of his robe. "I died in that battle. Celestia had begged Ashhur to make peace. He should have listened. The two gods fought once more as I remained a rotting body."

The fire between the two suddenly roared with life. Its flames danced in the air far above their heads. Amongst the fire's flickering tails, Qurrah saw images take shape. They were scattered and random, without time or order. He saw a small town besieged by corpses. He saw massive armies of undead marching across the plains to battle a horde of hyena-men. He saw the walls of a great city smashed to pieces as men climbed over, swords high and armor shining. And then he saw Karak and Ashhur cross blades.

He tore his eyes from the fire, unable to withstand the strength of the image. The fire shrank back to a small blaze.

"Most men cowered at the sight of it. Do not be ashamed," Velixar said. "There might have been a victor, but Celestia interfered at last. She cast each god far beyond the sky, to where she herself had made a home. She gave half to Ashhur and half to Karak. The souls of the soldiers who fought and died alongside them were given to their masters. She cursed the elves who sided with Karak, branding them the 'orcs,' or 'betrayers' in her tongue. Once the brother gods were locked away from the world, and each other, Celestia issued her final decree."

"What was it?" asked Qurrah after Velixar remained quiet for a moment.

"She ordered that Ashhur and Karak continue the fight they refused to end for all eternity. Many centuries have passed, Qurrah. I am the hilt of Karak's sword, the greatest priest in the war against Ashhur, and I have not relinquished my position."

The man's eyes grew so bright that the half-orc felt the urge to grovel.

"Ashhur himself killed me. Karak brought me back. He cursed those who had failed him, changing his realm into the abyss. I was the only one he spared, and he gave me life with all of his dwindling power."

The two sat in silence as the fire crackled between them. Qurrah dwelt on all he had heard, trying to decide what he believed. Strange as it seemed to him, he accepted every word.

"So what the priests say of how Karak is the god of death and darkness," Qurrah asked, "is it true?"

Velixar's eyes narrowed, and that vicious snarl returned.

"There were good men and evil men in his abyss after the war. The punishment was not to be eternal, not then, but Celestia chose Ashhur over my master." Qurrah watched as Velixar's hands clenched so tight his nails dug deep into his skin. Flesh tore, but no blood surfaced. "She took all who were good out of the abyss and gave their care to Ashhur. Left with nothing but thieves and murderers, Karak had no choice but to make it eternal. The abyss is dark, Qurrah, and there is fire, but there is also order."

"What do you wish of me?" Qurrah asked. Velixar's face softened into a dark smile.

"To fight the war. Celestia may have condemned it to continue forever, but she slumbers now. Harnessing enough power, we can defeat the goddess. We can bring all of Dezrel under our control and declare victory for Karak."

Qurrah stood, his eyes glimmering with anticipation. "Where will we strike first?"

"Woodhaven is a symbol of cooperation between races. That must be ended. We will burn Veldaren to ash thereafter. Once all of Neldar is in chaos, we may proceed however we wish."

"Will we strike the elves?" Qurrah asked.

"Why do you ask?"

The half-orc laughed.

"Mother was an orc who had lived here in Woodhaven. I do not know her name, other than what she instructed my brother and I to call her: Mama Tun. Our father was from Woodhaven, she told us. We later found out he was an elf, bizarre as it seems."

"It is a wretched elf who would mate with an orc," Velixar said.

"No true elf would," Qurrah said. "This means he was weak to have done so. His weakness has seeped into my blood."

"You hold no weakness," the man in black said. "The blood of orcs and elves is more similar than either race would care to admit. What happened to your mother?"

"I don't know. I was sold," he said, his face visibly darkening.

"To whom?"

"I was never given his name," Qurrah said. His voice, already soft and quiet, grew even quieter. "He was Master. That was all that mattered."

"Tell me of your time with Master," Velixar ordered.

"There is little to tell," Qurrah said. "I was his slave. I cleaned up after him while he fed me scraps of his failed experiments. I slept in a cage. One time he caught me practicing words of magic. As punishment, he shoved a hot poker down my throat, ruining my voice into what you hear now. One night tribes of hyena-men stormed his tower, wanting vengeance for the many of their kind he had taken to butcher and maim."

Qurrah kept his eyes low, unable to meet Velixar's gaze.

"I was afraid when they came, but as I watched Master slaughter hundreds of them with his golems and his shields of bone I felt at home amid the carnage. I knew then what I was to become."

"How did you escape?" Velixar asked.

"Master exhausted himself defending his tower," Qurrah said, waving a dismissive hand. "He collapsed at the very top. I cast a spell upon his throat, filling it with ice. I watched him die and then I left that disgusting place forever."

"You were a worthy apprentice," Velixar said. "Especially to learn such a spell on your own. Your master was blind."

"He was weakened," Qurrah said. "Even the clumsiest of fighters can slay a sleeping man."

"How old were you then?" Velixar asked.

"Nine," Qurrah said.

The man in black shook his head. His expression showed there would be no further argument. "If you had been mine at the age of nine... my previous apprentice Xelrak held but a shred of your strength."

Qurrah straightened at the name. "I have heard of Xelrak. He toppled the Citadel."

Velixar smiled as he remembered a cherished memory. "Indeed. It was his finest hour, and a significant victory for Karak. The paladins of Ashhur are all but crushed."

"What happened to him?"

His burning eyes held no kindness when the man in black spoke.

"Xelrak failed. Despite all the power I granted him, he failed. He tried to destroy the Council of Mages, but they destroyed him instead." Velixar gave a greedy look at Qurrah. "He was but a starving boy when I found him. I gave him a name and lent him my power. It is how I have survived all these centuries. I do not risk my own life, choosing instead to givemy power to others. I am the hilt, and my apprentice is the blade. But you..."

Again that greedy look.

"You are extraordinary. I do not have to give you unearned power. I must simply guide and instruct." Velixar stood, and when his power flared, Qurrah fell to his knees and worshipped his new master. "You are what I have searched for all these years. You and I will destroy this world side by side. We will lay waste to all life and put absolute order upon every last soul."

"Teach me," Qurrah said, his mouth buried into the dirt. "Show me the power I have sought for so very long."

Velixar looked down at his thin, ragged apprentice. "Rise. Let us begin."

Velixar taught until the stars retreated from the obnoxious sun. Qurrah returned home, his eyes sagging and his mind exhausted. When he climbed into bed, he fell asleep instantly. Not long after, Harruq rose, took his swords, and left for his own meeting.

"**Y**ou're late," Aurelia said, stepping out from behind a tree. Harruq shrugged and held out two branches he had whittled into crude imitations of swords.

"Had to make something for me to spar you with," he said.

"Those sticks are unnecessary," Aurelia said as she took up her staff, the tiniest hint of a smile curling on her lips. "Draw your swords."

"Are you sure?" Harruq asked, raising an eyebrow and gesturing to her completely unarmored figure. "I'll only end up hurting you."

"You won't," she said. "Here. Strike me with your blade."

The half-orc's jaw dropped a little. "You've lost your mind?"

"I said hit me, orc!" Aurelia shouted.

Harruq snarled, and out came his weapons. He swung for her face, turning the blade at the last moment so the flat side struck her. The sword smacked off Aurelia's cheek as if she were made of stone. The clear noise rang throughout the forest.

"What the abyss was that?" Harruq asked.

Aurelia laughed. "I've cast an enchantment that protects me from your blades."

Harruq looked at his weapons and then shrugged. "Interesting. Do I get one too?"

In answer, Aurelia smacked her staff against Harruq's shin. The half-orc roared in pain as he hopped up and down on one foot.

"Damn it!" he shouted. "What was that for?"

"Hitting you is my reward for doing well," she said. "Consider it my way of making sure you don't go easy on me. So are you ready to begin?"

Harruq mumbled something obscene. He nodded, swinging in a low chop. As his sword struck her staff, the sparring began.

Aurelia was familiar with her staff, the wood comfortable in her grip. She had no sense of tactic, though, and all it took was a quick feint or two before she left herself horribly open.

Harruq used only one sword, running it in slow circles, stabs, and the occasional feint. He enjoyed the steady workout but savored even more watching Aurelia move gracefully through the air. Whenever his eyes lingered too long, however, he'd feel the sharp sting of Aurelia's staff against his arms or chest.

When they finished, Harruq slumped onto his rear and rubbed his bruises.

"I shouldn't be able to hit you," Aurelia said as she sat across from him, her legs tucked underneath her.

"Yeah, so?" Harruq asked.

"So tomorrow don't let me hit you," she said.

The half-orc mumbled and rolled his eyes. Aurelia leaned back against a tree, her eyes studying him. Her look gave him shivers, both good and bad.

"Tell me about yourself," she said. Harruq raised an eyebrow. "Your childhood. Your likes. Your life."

"For what reason?" he asked.

"I heard those men. I saved you from the gallows. I would prefer to know more about the life I spared."

Harruq leaned his head on his fist and stared at the grass, growing increasingly uncomfortable. "I don't know. Not too much to tell really. My brother and I grew up in Veldaren, and about three months ago the king kicked out all elves. Believe it or not, that included us."

Aurelia grabbed his sleeve to halt him. "First, who is your brother? Second, since when are you elvish?"

The half-orc chuckled, but still kept his eyes downward. "Our mum was an orc. Dad was an elf. Never met dad, and mum sold Qurrah and me when we were both little. I ran away and lived on the streets of Veldaren. Found Qurrah about a year or two later, hiding in the streets after he escaped his master. My brother, well…"

She watched as Harruq struggled through some sort of internal debate. His brown eyes finally rose to meet hers.

"Qurrah's like you, but not. You can cast magic right?" Aurelia nodded. "Well, he can too. But he… he's different. When we were kids, he found a little mouse. It was dead as dead can be. He closed his hands around it, just like this, and then whispered some words he learned from secretly watching Master."

"Master?" Aurelia asked, interrupting him again.

"Yeah," Harruq said, frowning. "My brother didn't have too much fun before I found him. We were both sold, but I escaped. Qurrah, though, he was sold to Master…forget it, that's for another time. All that matters is that he learned those words before he met me. He whispered something, opened his hands, and then just like that the mouse got up and started running."

"He brought it to life?" she asked.

"Well…" Again he stopped, obviously uneasy about what he wanted to say. "It was still dead, but it was moving now. That make sense? Qurrah could make it do whatever he wanted. He let it run off and die, that first one he showed me. He was pretty shy about it. Don't think he had any idea how I would react."

Harruq suddenly stopped and laughed. "You should have seen us, Aurelia. We spent the rest of the day chasing after mice so we could stomp them and have Qurrah bring them back to do tricks."

Aurelia smiled at the burly half-orc.

"You really made them do tricks?" she asked.

"Well, yeah, some jumps and flips. We tried to see how high we could make one climb before… what?"

She was smiling, but when pressed she refused to answer him. Instead, she stood, brushed off her dress, and flipped her hair over her shoulders. "Same time tomorrow?" she asked.

"Sure," Harruq said. "But how many times will we be doing this?"

Aurelia shrugged. "Until I feel you have paid me back."

"So what, a couple days?"

"You know very well I can't obtain any proficiency in such a short time," she said.

Harruq shrugged. "Fine then," he said. "How long you want me stuck here with you?"

"Two weeks," she said. The elf danced away behind a tree. Harruq followed, but all he caught when he stepped around was a tiny line of blue fading on the afternoon wind.

"That was interesting," he said before returning to Woodhaven.

Deeper in the forest, Aurelia stepped out of a glowing blue portal. An elf waited there, an ornate bow slung across his back.

"So do you think it could be him?" he asked her.

"Perhaps," Aurelia said. "I think it's in him. Something is wrong, though. He's too light hearted, too free."

"What does that mean?" the other elf asked, his fingers twitching at the string of his bow.

"I don't know, Dieredon." Aurelia sighed. "It means he's capable, but would not do so without reason. If he's butchering the children, he's doing it for someone else."

"Who?" Dieredon asked.

She shrugged. "My guess is his brother. He sounds like a necromancer."

Dieredon nodded. "I'll find him and watch him for a bit. If either of them slaughters another child, I will see it and put an end to it."

Aurelia pulled a few strands of hair away from her mouth and tucked them behind her ear.

"This seems like a small matter for a scoutmaster to be involved. Are you sure you have nothing more important to do?"

"Murdered human children?" Dieredon shrugged. "Let the humans and orcs do as they wish, but when they butcher their young they must be made to suffer. You were right to contact me, Aurelia."

"I hope so," Aurelia said. "I saw one of the bodies, and what was done to him, those vile carvings…"

Dieredon kissed her forehead.

"Put it behind you so you may focus on the task at hand. If the half-orcs are guilty, they will make a mistake soon enough. Your eyes and ears are vital in confirming their guilt."

"I'll try to keep him talking," Aurelia said. "And I'll find out more about his brother. I hope I can bear Harruq's company in the meanwhile. He can be quite a brute sometimes."

"Come now," Dieredon said, his face suddenly brightening into a smile. "He sounds like a real fine man to me. I wouldn't be surprised if you two got married. Perhaps a kid or three. Little gray-skinned Aurrys crawling over the forest, wouldn't that be cute?"

She smacked him with her staff and then teleported away, leaving Dieredon to laugh long after her departure.

"Where did you get the bruises?" Qurrah asked when Harruq returned to their squalid home.

"Practicing," Harruq said. "We have anything to eat?"

His brother motioned to a small plate of bacon and some eggs still in their shells.

"Wonderful."

The smaller half-orc watched his brother wolf down the meal.

"Would you accompany me into madness?" he asked. Harruq gave him a funny look, half a piece of bacon still hanging in his mouth.

"Of course I would," he replied. "If you go mad, I've got no chance in this world. You brains, me brawn, right?"

"Yes," Qurrah said absently. "That's right. But would you kill? Without reason, without pause. Could you?"

Harruq cracked open an egg and swallowed it raw.

"Don't I do so already?" he asked. "If I had to pick between the world and you, the entire world would be a bloody mess."

He swallowed the other egg, wiped his mouth on his sleeve, and burped.

"Well put, Harruq," Qurrah said.

5

"Did you practice the spells I taught you?" Velixar asked as Qurrah took his seat by the fire.

"Yes," Qurrah said. "I am more than pleased with them."

"You will need to keep a fresh supply of bones with you," Velixar said, reaching into his pouch. "Take these for now until you can obtain more."

Qurrah accepted the bones, stashing them into a small pocket he had sewn onto his robe. A silence fell over the two as far away a wolf howled.

"I wonder," Velixar said, gazing in the direction of the howl. "Do you have a brother?"

Qurrah shifted his weight a bit. "Why do you ask?"

Velixar looked up to the moon and stared as he spoke.

"I have had dreams. I see you beside me, a strong ally, but I see another half-orc leading my army. He is strong and wields two enormous swords. Again I ask, do you have a brother?"

Qurrah pulled out a bone from his pouch and stared at it.

"I do," he said. "You wish for him to help?"

"He will do more than aid us," Velixar whispered to the moon. "His power is as great as yours, Qurrah. You two are vessels of possibility unseen in centuries. It is as if one of the gods had a hand in your creation."

Qurrah chuckled. "If any god had a hand in creating us, we were forgotten soon after. We both have suffered, I more than Harruq. We never had a home or a family. By will alone we survived. There is nothing special about us, not even our blood."

"And that is why you are strong," the man in black said, his lips ever-changing. "All things are for a reason. Even those who dwell in the darkness such as I will not deny this truth. You were meant for me. I will train you, and you will aid me in sundering all that brings false stability to this chaotic world."

"For death and power," Qurrah whispered.

"For Karak," Velixar corrected. "When can I meet your brother?"

The half-orc shrugged. While he seemed calm, the man in black did not miss how his eyes still refused to meet his.

"Give me time," Qurrah said. "Let me make sure he is ready."

"Is he not open to Karak?" Velixar asked.

"He is open," Qurrah said a bit too vehemently. A glare from Velixar calmed him before he continued. "My brother can be a mindless butcher, but he must be angered or spurned into battle. When peaceful, his mind entertains ideas that run... contrary to what he and I are."

"And what is that, Qurrah? What are you and your brother?"

The fire sparked a shower of orange into the sky as Qurrah spoke.

"Superior."

In the distance, elven eyes watched that cough of flame stretch to the stars, as well as the sight of those two huddled figures talking long through the night.

◁◈▷

The first week of training went well for both Harruq and Aurelia. The half-orc kept on the offensive, determined not to add a fresh set of bruises to his body. Aurelia still fell for the feints, however slow, but her blocks were already quicker and more precise. They fought until both collapsed against trees, sweat soaking their bodies.

"You're starting to get the hang of it," Harruq said after their fifth session.

"Don't flatter me," Aurelia said, refastening one of her braids that had come loose. "You're still going too easy."

"If I move too fast you won't learn anything," Harruq insisted.

"How do you know?" she asked. "Do you train elves often?"

The half-orc grinned. "All the time. I'm known for it, in fact. Harruq Tun, trainer of elves, slayer of dragons, and man of the ladies."

"Please." She rolled her eyes. "Not this lady."

"Never said you were one, elfie."

Aurelia gave Harruq a brutal glare. "And why not?"

He picked at some grass and said nothing.

"Well?" she asked.

"Well what?" He looked up, his face blank and his eyes wide as if he hadn't a clue.

"Why am I not a lady?" Aurelia asked.

"I don't know," Harruq said. "Did you cast a spell on yourself or something? Look like one to me."

She stood and took up her staff. Instead of grabbing his swords, Harruq ducked behind a tree.

"Don't hurt me," he shouted. His face poked around the tree, his long brown hair falling down past his eyes. Much as she tried not to, Aurelia burst into laughter.

"Get over here," she said.

A small silver dagger appeared in her hands. Harruq eyed it warily.

"What's that for?" he asked.

"When was the last time you cut your hair?" Aurelia asked.

The half-orc shrugged, for some reason embarrassed. "I don't know. I just hack it off with a sword if it ever gets to be a bother. Been awhile, though."

"It shows." The elf motioned to the grass before her. "Sit, and tell me another of your wonderful stories while I make you look less like an animal."

Harruq grumbled, but when she frowned and crossed her arms the normal defiance in him melted away. He plopped down and sighed.

"Something must be wrong with me," he said.

"Shut up and start telling me more about yourself."

"Huh?"

"Just do it."

So the half-orc shut up, paused, shrugged, and then began.

"Well, this isn't a happy tale, but it's the only one I can think of. It's about a present Qurrah gave me. He's a softie at times, and this is one of them times."

Aurelia smoothed his hair in her fingers, frowned, and then sliced off a large chunk with the incredibly sharp dagger. Brown hair fell in clumps at Harruq's feet.

"You're going to leave me some up there, right?" he asked.

"Don't make me cut your ears," Aurelia warned.

Harruq began his story. He told her of a gift from his brother, a tiny sword Qurrah had whittled from bone. A bully had stolen it, but then Qurrah used a dead rat under his control to steal it back while they slept.

The haircut and the story ended at the same time. Dirty hair was strewn over the grass.

"Never had much," Harruq said. "That bone sword was my only possession. Still had to hide it because of that bully. You know, it's probably still there, buried underneath our home."

"You and your brother had such rough beginnings," Aurelia said, tucking away the dagger. "Very rough."

Harruq shrugged. "Never seemed a big deal to us. Others were better off. A few were worse. We did what we had to live, just like everybody else."

He ran a hand through his now shoulder-length hair, shaking away loose strands. It felt odd having so little hair on his head. Aurelia sat down on her legs, her hands folded upon her dress.

"Harruq, have you killed before?" she asked.

The half-orc opened his mouth and then closed it. A boy's face flashed before his eyes.

You're an orc, aren't you?

"Yes," he said at last. "I've killed."

He eyed Aurelia, desperately wishing to know what she thought yet unable to figure out why he even cared. He thought he saw pity in her eyes, perhaps compassion. But there was a hardness there, a doubting that made him wonder just how much of him she truly knew.

"Tell me of the first time," she said.

He shook his head. "Not today. Maybe some other session, if I feel I can."

They both stood, Aurelia stepping away while Harruq stretched and popped his back.

"Goodbye Harruq," she said.

The elf was almost past the trees when he spoke. "Hey, Aurelia?"

"Yes, Harruq?" she said, turning to face him.

"Have you ever killed?"

She paused, and then ever so slightly nodded. The two parted without another word.

"**W**hat did you learn this time?" Dieredon asked as Aurelia arrived at their designated spot in the forest.

"Something is wrong," she told him. "He's kind-hearted, even goofy. He takes to his swordcraft with almost perfectionist precision. Everything else he does is for fun or survival." Aurelia sighed and rubbed her hands across her face.

"It could all be an act," Dieredon ventured. "Or just a side of his personality. Perhaps you see the elf in him. There are multiple sides to all men, for only the insane and the dull contain just one facet to their being. It could be Harruq's orcish side that pushes him to kill the children."

She nodded at the possibility. "I will defer to your wisdom. The more time I spend with him, the more I wonder. What about you? What have you learned?"

Dieredon's face darkened. "His brother worries me. I have seen him conversing at night with a strange man."

"Strange?" she asked. "How so?"

He chuckled. "It may sound odd, but I can see his eyes. They burn like fire. He dresses himself in the black robes of a priest, and I cannot find his tracks come the morning. That doesn't happen, Aurelia. If it moves, I can track it. And I can't find a thing."

"These two brothers are certainly a mystery," Aurelia said.

"When will you meet this other brother?" Dieredon asked.

"Qurrah?" Aurelia shrugged. "When Harruq is ready for us to meet."

"Very well. I will continue tracking them. There have been no murders for the past few days. It seems our warnings have worked, for now."

Aurelia smiled. "Praise Celestia for that. May she watch over you, Dieredon."

"And you as well, Aurelia Thyne," he replied.

"**C**lear your mind," Velixar said to his apprentice. "Let the emptiness give you comfort."

The wind blew, swirling cold through his ragged clothes. Velixar watched his apprentice take several deep breaths.

"For this spell to work, you must have a significant idea in mind," he said. "Make it bleak and vile. If you are to darken someone's dreams, your own mind must be just as dark."

Qurrah breathed out, his eyelids fluttering as a memory surfaced in his meditation.

"Send the image to me, my apprentice. Let me have the anger, the darkness, and the despair."

Velixar lurched backward as the memory rammed into his mind. Qurrah was unpracticed, and his delivery brutal. Still, the vision did come, clouded and chaotic.

A gang of children slept on a stack of hay. They were filthy, scrawny, and diseased. A small rat crept near, its mouth covered with flecks of white foam. When close enough, it latched onto the hand of the biggest child, who awoke screaming. Time distorted so that days passed as that scream lingered. His face paled, his mouth foamed, and then he died, screaming, still screaming.

The vision ended. Velixar opened his eyes.

"What is it that I saw?" he asked.

"The second time I ever killed," Qurrah said. "I watched that wretched bully succumb to madness from the disease carried by an undead rat. He took something I made for my brother, and I made him pay dearly for it."

The man in black nodded, going over the memory in his mind.

"Could be darker, though," he said. "You need not use memories, but they are easier to project. Any thought can be sent to those who slumber. After you have practiced, we will try with images you created on your own."

The half-orc pulled his robes around him and looked back to the city. "When will we assault Woodhaven?" he asked.

Velixar's face was an unmoving stone. "When did I say we would?"

"When we first met," Qurrah said. "You said the cooperation between the races needs to end. If we are to destroy our home, I must know when."

Then Velixar did something completely unexpected. He laughed.

"It will not be our hands that destroy Woodhaven," Velixar said. "King Vaelor will do so for us by starting a war that will give us the dead we need."

"How?" Qurrah asked.

The fire burned in Velixar's eyes, deep with anticipation.

"I will darken his dreams, just as I have shown you. He is a cowardly man, and fears the elves already. I played a large part in his decision to banish the elves from the city. After I'm done, he will want them gone from all his lands, including here."

The man in black gestured to the city nestled against the forest.

"This city has long been treated neutral, even though it resides within Neldar's border. The elves will not take kindly to removal from a home many have lived in since before our dear king's grandparents were alive."

"I eagerly await the bloodshed," Qurrah said. He bowed to his master.

"Go. The night is young. Taint the dreams of the slumbering."

Qurrah left Velixar to sit alone before the fire. The dark night sang a song of crickets and wind. In the quiet, Dieredon entered the light of the fire.

"Greetings, traveler," the elf said, bowing. "The town is not far, and all are welcome. Would you not sleep in safety rather than in the wild?"

Velixar looked at the elf, dressed in camouflaged armor and holding his wicked bow.

"You are a scoutmaster for the Quellan elves, are you not?" he asked.

"I am. And you have remained outside our village for several days yet vanish with the morning sun."

"Have I done something wrong?" Velixar asked.

Dieredon frowned, noticing the subtle yet constant changes to the man's facial features. His instincts cried out in warning. This man was dangerous.

"Children have been dying in our forest, all found horribly butchered," Dieredon said.

"As you can plainly see, I am nowhere near the forest," Velixar said. His voice was calm, disarming. Dieredon did not buy it.

"Give me your name," he said.

"Earn the privilege," Velixar countered. The elf's arms blurred, and then the bow was in his hands. He pulled no arrow, though, for he held the weapon much like one would hold a staff.

"Leave this place," Dieredon ordered as two long blades snapped out of either side of the bow and many spikes punched out the front. The man in black rose to his feet, an aura of death and despair rolling out around him.

"You should not threaten those who can rip the bones from your body with a thought," he said, his voice dripping with venom.

"And you should not threaten an elf who can tear out your throat before a single word of a spell may pass through your lips. Go. Now."

"As you wish," Velixar said, giving a low, mocking bow. Then he was gone, fading away like smoke on a strong wind. Dieredon sprinted back to Woodhaven, knowing that the darkness was no longer safe to him.

6

Ome sword came from above, aiming for her shoulder, while the other thrust low. The staff twirled, batting the thrust to one side. Aurelia spun, evading a downward strike slicing through the air by just an inch. She continued the turn, her staff whirling. The swords sliced, trying to block, but they were too slow. The staff cracked against Harruq's forehead.

He staggered backward, his eyes going wide and blank.

"You could fell an ogre with that hit," he said.

"Very funny," Aurelia said. She smiled. "That was my first good hit of the day. Mind if we make it the last?"

"I'm doomed," Harruq said, ignoring her. "Oh, the agony. What a way to die." He collapsed, his arms splayed wide and his tongue hanging out of his mouth.

Aurelia giggled. "Never thought a half-orc dying could be so adorable."

His eyes flared wide.

"I'm not!" he insisted.

She slid over beside him, her long hair cascading toward his face.

"Oh, but I think you are," she said. "Since you're down here, how about I--"

"I'm fine. I'm fine." Harruq sat up, breathing heavily even though the sparring match had been relatively casual. The elf smirked and trotted away.

"Hey, Aurelia," Harruq said.

"Yes, Harruq?" She turned around.

Harruq tapped his fingers against the hilts of his swords and glanced about the clearing.

"I...you still want to hear that story?" he asked.

The playful atmosphere vanished into the trees. Aurelia returned and sat on her heels. She placed a hand on his shoulder. He tensed and jerked away, then blushed at his reaction.

"Sorry," Harruq stood up, his face burning red. "This is stupid. I'm leaving."

"Stay, please," Aurelia said. The half-orc halted, turned, and sat back down. His face was still beet red but the elf paid it no mind.

"Alright," Harruq grumbled. "No interrupting, and no saying a thing. I just want to get this over with. Don't even know why I'm telling you this."

"Because you must," she said, a bit of her stubbornness returning. "Because I need to know."

The half-orc nodded. He began his story.

"The only money I ever made was working for the king," Harruq said. "This was after the orcs attacked Veldaren about a year ago and busted up the walls. They were hiring everybody to help rebuild and I was just as strong then as I am now. They weren't paying much, but you got to remember we were stealing food to live. Those few coins they gave me were a treasure.

"Most didn't mind me working with 'em. I worked hard, harder than most, and I kept my mouth shut if you can believe it. Only one guy there hated me, and I mean hated. Perry was his name. Always calling me names, trying to make me lose my balance while lifting and carrying things. Then he did something stupid, Aurelia. He did that in front of Qurrah."

Harruq thrust out his chin and squinted.

"This was how that Perry guy looked. Seen dogs look more human. He was strong, and I think he was the strongest before I showed up. I told him about this contest me and Qurrah made up, some arm wrestling thing. Guy was drunk out of his mind, so when I told him we could win four gold coins he should have figured something was off.

"We met after work, just past sundown, and I led him straight to Qurrah, who cast a spell on Perry then, kind of like you did with the guards. He shouted until his head turned purple but made no sound for the effort. Then Qurrah cast another spell that made him go all tough and rigid. Felt like I was holding a stick. We took him inside and put him on the floor.

"He wasn't supposed to die," Harruq said, staring right into Aurelia's eyes so she would know he spoke the truth. "We didn't mean to have what happened happen, but well... Qurrah put a bunch of meat on Perry's face. It was old and rancid. Poor guy still had to keep smelling it though, and then Qurrah cast his spell.

"The meat started bubbling and turning watery. It ran down his face, getting into his eyes. It burned him. His skin turned black, like it was rotting. He called me dogface all the time, Perry did. We were making him just like what he called me. A dogface. But it went wrong. I yelled at Qurrah to stop, and I think he wanted to, but he kept shrieking more of that curse. Then he..."

Harruq rubbed his eyes and refused to meet Aurelia's gaze.

"And then Qurrah removed the spells that kept him from talking and moving. He screamed and screamed and he just, he just...he tore off his own face. He reached up and yanked that mess off him. He died. Qurrah fell over, too weak to stand. Never seen him so scared in my life. He kept staring at that guy's face and blubbering, saying he didn't mean to. That's all he said, over and over. He didn't mean to. He tried to stop. We burned the body and haven't ever talked about it since."

Silence filled their clearing as Harruq's story ended.

"I asked for the first time you killed," Aurelia said after an agonizingly long pause.

"I know," Harruq said. "And I did. I brought Perry to Qurrah. I failed to stop him when I saw something was wrong. If there is blame, it falls on me."

The elf stared off into the forest, her brown eyes seeing nothing. Harruq and Qurrah's relationship could not be clearer to her mind. Qurrah directed, Qurrah ordered, and then Harruq bore the guilt and the blame. Did Harruq ever consider disobedience? She didn't know.

"We done here?" the half-orc asked.

He left without giving her a chance to answer.

The final days of sparring with Aurelia passed quietly and swiftly. Aurelia asked for no stories and Harruq told her none. They simply enjoyed each other's company, fought to the extent of their skill, and then parted. On the fourteenth and final day, however, Harruq was in an unusually quiet mood. His mind refused to stay on the mock combat, and many times a quick jab of Aurelia's staff cracked his arm or wrist when he should have easily deflected it away.

Finally, the elf called it a day. She set aside her staff.

"I thank you for sparring with me," she told him.

"It's nothing," he said. "Better to spar with someone than practice alone."

Aurelia smiled. "You're different than what I expected, Harruq. Smarter, too."

Harruq blushed. "No need for lies," he said.

The elf laughed a little but said nothing. Instead, she walked over and gave Harruq a quick peck on the cheek.

"Keep your big butt safe, okay?" she said.

The half-orc tried to answer but his mouth refused to cooperate. Somehow, it seemed to have become unhinged. Besides, it wasn't as if he could think of anything to say. All his mind could concentrate on was the feel of the elf's soft lips on his cheek, the flowery scent of her perfume mixed with sweat, and the quick brush of her breasts against his arm.

By the time his jaw and mind began working again, Aurelia was laughing.

"What's so funny?" he demanded. The elf smiled.

"Nothing. Just a big stupid half-orc I'm going to miss. Bye-bye."

She waved and then vanished into the forest. For a long time, Harruq remained. He ran a hand through his hair and pondered what in the abyss was wrong with him.

"Never get involved with elves," he mumbled. "Never ever should have gotten myself screwed up like this."

But a part of him liked it, and that scared him even more.

❖

Harruq arrived at the clearing the next morning at the same time as always. Aurelia stepped out from behind a tree, her cold, emotionless face so different from the previous day.

"We have sparred our two weeks, Harruq," she said. "You have no need to come here."

"Yeah, well, you heard what I said yesterday," Harruq said, his face red.

"What was that?"

He kicked a rock. "It's better to spar with another, remember?"

Aurelia frowned. "You know I am a sorceress. My time should be spent studying my craft. I only wanted to be proficient with my staff, not a master."

A tiny bit of panic crept into Harruq's voice. "Yeah, but, but, it's only an hour or two, and who said you were proficient anyway? I could beat you without trying, and so could anyone better than me. It would be stupid now to just stop and…"

Aurelia crossed the distance between them and placed her hand across his mouth to shut him up. A grin lit her entire face.

"Okay, Harruq. I will do as you wish and keep meeting with you."

"For sparring," he said after she pulled her hand away.

"Sure. That too."

Harruq blushed but let it go.

"Well, you ready to go, little elfie?" he said, trying act gruff.

"Of course." Aurelia retrieved her staff, smiling to herself. The offer flattered her more than Harruq could know.

"Well," Aurelia said, twirling her staff. "Ready for a go?"

"Oh yeah," Harruq said, drawing his swords. "You've got no idea."

But she did, and it made her laugh all the more.

7

"It is time I met your brother," Velixar said as the clouds rolled above, obscuring the waning moon. He had trained with Qurrah for almost two months, and over that time the half-orc had grown greatly in power. "King Vaelor's nightmares have never been stronger, and he will act upon them soon."

"I am not sure Harruq is ready," Qurrah said. "It is difficult enough bringing me here. The two of us sneaking out each night might be noticed."

"You will draw no attention," Velixar said, ending the debate. "Bring him. Let him swear his life to me."

"As you wish, my master," Qurrah said with a bow.

"Hey Aurry, I got something for you!" Harruq tramped into the clearing, his two swords sheathed. Aurelia waited there, her arms crossed.

"A present from a half-orc," she said. "Should I be worried?"

"Nope. Just take it." He held out a small brown box. It was in poor shape, picked out of a heap of trash, but the elf could see the great care spent attempting to clean and fix it.

"What is inside?" she asked as she took the box.

"Open it," Harruq said. "You'll see."

Aurelia pried off the lid and peered inside. A small bouquet of flowers lay on the bottom of the box. She lifted them up, smiling at the violets, blues, and reds.

"That's sweet Harruq, but why?"

"Just to, you know." He kicked a rock. "Wanted to thank you for sparring with me," he said.

"They're beautiful," Aurelia said as she inhaled the aroma. "But why the box?"

Harruq turned a new shade of red. "Well, I'd look weird walking down the street with those flowers in hand. I do have a reputation to keep."

The elf laughed. "Thank you, Harruq. Are you ready to begin?"

He nodded, eager to have the awkwardness pass. Aurelia twirled the staff in her hands as her smile faded into seriousness. Harruq drew his swords, and then they sparred.

❖

"You're out later than normal," Qurrah said when Harruq returned to their home.

"I get restless stuck in here," he said. He dropped his weapons in the corner, shed much of his leather armor, and then released a loud groan as he settled down.

"Harruq, I must ask a favor of you," Qurrah said. He sat next to his brother.

"Sure thing," Harruq said. "What you need?"

Qurrah fiddled with the bones in his pouch. "There is someone I need you to meet."

Harruq raised an eyebrow. "The person you've been sneaking off to each night?" he asked.

"You know?" Qurrah asked.

"Course," he said, shrugging. "You're sneaky, brother, but I'm not as deep a sleeper as you think I am. So who is this person?"

Qurrah bit his lower lip. "His name is…he will tell you his name. He is powerful, Harruq. Very powerful. I've taken him as my teacher, and I want him to become yours as well."

Harruq raised his arms and flexed, watching his calloused hands open and close. "What can a teacher of magic offer me?" he asked.

Qurrah chuckled.

"You'd be surprised," he replied. "But will you accompany me tonight?"

"Fine, fine, I will," he said.

"You will impress him, Harruq, do not worry about that."

Qurrah left his brother to rest.

"Grab my wrist," Qurrah said as the dark cloud arrived that night. Harruq did so, and together they stepped inside. He felt an unseen hand grab his chest, and then they were running blind. The minutes crawled, their frantic breathing the only audible sound. Qurrah lagged further and further behind, unable to keep the pace. Harruq tightened his grip on his wrist and pulled him along. The terrain sloped beneath them as they climbed a hill. Another quick shift and they were stumbling down that same hill. The cold hand vanished. The cloud dissipated. Before him, standing with his arms crossed, waited Velixar.

Qurrah stunned his brother by falling to one knee and bowing his head.

"Greetings, master," Qurrah said. "I have brought him as you asked."

Delighted, Velixar grinned as he surveyed the tall, muscular half-orc. As with Qurrah, he saw the untapped potential, incredible strength, and skill waiting for a purpose to harness it. The subtle shift of Velixar's features slowed as he approached. When he spoke in his deep, rumbling voice, Harruq struggled against a sudden urge to join his brother on one knee.

"So you are Harruq?" the man in black asked.

"I am," Harruq said.

Velixar reached out a hand. It was frail, bony. So similar to his brother's.

"Kneel."

Harruq did so unwillingly.

"I am Velixar," he continued. "I am the voice of Karak. I've heard much about you, Harruq Tun, bastard child of an orcish womb. You are strong, and I sense your anger raging to be unleashed."

Harruq trembled, indeed feeling that anger. He felt it deep inside his chest, urging him to rise and defy Velixar.

"The orcish were elves who swore their lives to Karak. Part of you still yearns to do what your ancestors have done. They reveled in bloodshed, warred against men who followed a false god. I offer you a chance to do as you were meant to and serve Karak. Answer me this question, half-orc. Do you love your brother?"

A chill ran through his spine. He glanced to Qurrah, who still knelt. His eyes were focused on him. In them, he saw pride.

"Aye, I do," Harruq said. "I would do anything for him."

Velixar let his hand slowly lower until his fingertips hovered before Harruq's forehead.

"Then I ask you this: will you devote your life to the protection of his? Will you swear your life to me, as your brother has? I can guide you, teach you, and give you the power to protect him. Answer me."

Harruq looked once more at his brother and then let his head fall.

"I swear my life to you. And to Qurrah."

"I would have it no other way," Velixar said.

A hand touched his forehead. All the anger that had raged inside Harruq roared like a fire suddenly loosed upon a dry forest. Sweat poured from his skin. His head jerked upward, his eyes soaking in the white of Velixar's hand and the dim glow of the stars. Power flowed into him, his muscles stretching and tightening in a chaotic manner.

"Rise, Harruq Tun," Velixar said. "Revel in the power of Karak."

"By the gods, brother, if you could see yourself," Qurrah said, his voice full of shock and wonder.

"Just one god, Qurrah," Velixar corrected. "All this by the hand of one. I am that hand."

Harruq stood and looked down. His arms and legs bulged with muscle. He flexed his arm and stared at the growth that traveled all the way up to his neck. He felt within himself a lifewell of energy, one infinitely deep.

"Discard your swords, Harruq," Velixar said. "You are the protector of my disciple. You deserve better."

He slid his two swords out from their sheaths, stunned by the ease in which he moved them. It was if they went from being made of steel to air. He tossed them aside. Velixar pulled from within his cloak a chest the size of a small stone. He placed it on the grass where it shone gold in the light of the stars. As the two brothers watched, he whispered a few words of magic, enlarging the chest to normal size.

"Over the centuries, I have gathered many items to aid those who would swear their lives to me," Velixar said. The locks clicked open, the lid raised, and then he reached inside and pulled out two swords sheathed in gleaming obsidian. "These swords were once wielded by Aerland Shen. He led the elves that aided Karak in the great war against Ashhur. When Celestia cursed his kind, they shared his curse." Velixar smiled at Harruq, his eyes gleaming.

"Long have I waited for someone to wield these blades. An elf crafted and used them in battle, an elf cursed into an orc. These swords can only be held by one who has the blood of both inside him." Velixar held the hilts out to Harruq, who drew one from its sheath. The sword's blade was deep black and wreathed in a soft red glow. He weaved it through the air, his mouth agape at the ease in which it glided.

"They are not as long as your previous weapons," Velixar said, "but you will adjust. These blades will make you faster and more skillful than ever before. Forget everything you know about yourself, and know only that you are unstoppable."

Harruq took the other sword and held both in his hands. He noticed the writing that flared on each hilt, one red, the other gold.

"What do they say?" he asked, staring at them in wonder.

"Condemnation and Salvation. You are judgment, Harruq. May it be swift and merciless."

Harruq sheathed the swords and clipped them to his belt. He knelt as his head swirled.

"Thank you, master."

"None are more deserving," Qurrah said, putting an arm on his brother's shoulder.

"There is one, and it is you, Qurrah," Velixar said. He pulled out one item more before closing the chest and shrinking it back to its original size. In his hand remained a long black whip that curled about as if alive.

"Weapons may not be your preference, but I trust you will find some use for this."

As both brothers watched, the whip burst into flame. Velixar cracked it once to the grass, instantly charring the green earth into ash.

"Why?" Qurrah asked.

"Magic is not your greatest weapon, my disciple. Fear and pain are, and this whip is capable of producing both."

The fire died as the whip wound itself around Velixar's arm like a snake. He held it out to Qurrah, who took it with great reverence.

"With but a thought it will strike as you wish," his master told him. "Let it learn your heart, and you will find it more than sufficient." Velixar held out his arms and smiled at the two half-orc brothers. They both knelt before him, basking in his unhidden power. "It is time you used these gifts. Not far is a small village. Go to it. Slaughter everyone without exception."

Harruq's muscles screamed for use. He could barely register the request asked of him. All he could think of was wielding his swords in battle.

"Which way do we go?" he asked.

"I know the way," Qurrah said, his eyes lingering on the whip curled about his right arm. "Their nightmares are crying out to me. You have prepared them, haven't you master?"

The man in black nodded. "They know death is coming. So go."

Qurrah bowed once more and then began walking west. Harruq followed.

As the two left his sight Velixar broke out in hysterical laughter.

"Yes, I do believe the time has come," the man said to his master. "Celestia has faltered greatly to let them fall into our hands." He paused, listening to the soft whisper of Karak in his mind. "Perhaps. With Qurrah's magic as strong as it is, I have an ally worthy of your name. All of Neldar will burn, and thereafter, you will have your freedom!"

Velixar traveled west, following unseen after his two apprentices. He would witness their first true test, and he would bask in the bloodshed that was sure to come.

The two traveled over the gentle hills, only the rough gasps of Qurrah's breathing breaking the silence. As the two neared the village, Harruq dared to speak.

"Qurrah," he asked, "who is this Velixar?"

"He is a teacher," the half-orc whispered in between ragged breaths. "One wiser than I ever thought possible."

"So we'll do what he says? We'll kill the village, all of them, without reason?"

Qurrah stopped their progress by turning and placing his hands on his brother's shoulders. His eyes burned into Harruq's, so strong in force that the larger brother could not look away.

"You have done much for me without question, without pause. This is different. Velixar has given us the power and privilege to do what we were always meant to do. I need you to embrace this. Velixar's reason is the only reason we need, that we will ever need. It is in our blood, our orcish blood, and that is a weight even your muscles cannot hold back. We are killers, murderers, butchers, now granted purpose within that. That is our fate. That is our reason. Do you understand?"

Harruq's fingers traced the hilts of his new swords. He knew what his brother asked. He had killed before, but this was different. This was a complete surrender to the murderer within. He thought of his vow to Velixar, and also to his brother. Obedience. Loyalty. He had sworn his entire life to them. What else did he know? What else could he be?

He thought of Aurelia only once before he spoke. Her face was a white knife in the darkness of his mind, and he buried her deep within his heart as he yielded to the wisdom of his brother.

"Yeah," Harruq said. "I understand."

"Good. Now come." The two resumed traveling up the small hill. They stopped again, however, for from their vantage point they could see the village.

"See the torches?" Harruq asked, pointing. His brother nodded.

"Velixar's nightmares have pulled them from their slumber. It would be too easy otherwise."

"It's going to be easy anyway," Harruq said, drawing his blades. The soft red glow splashed across their faces.

"Are you ready, brother?"

"I am," he lied. "Let's go."

8

Jeremiah Stoutmire walked through the village of Cornrows, the hair on his neck erect. The cool spring breeze was weak compared to the ice that locked his spine. He held a torch in one hand and a shortsword in the other. At first, he had thought himself foolish waking in a full panic from a nightmare he could not remember. Then he saw others about, lit torches in their hands, and he knew his fear was justified. A young, fat-nosed farmer saw him awake and approached.

"Couldn't sleep either, Jeremiah?" he asked.

"Aye, had the worst nightmares." Jeremiah glanced at the sword in the farmer's hand. "You feel the same, don't you?"

The farmer nodded.

"Feels like the dark god himself is coming for us. Part of me wants to grab my children and run."

"Perhaps it is a warning," Jeremiah said. "Ashhur may be granting us a chance. Bandits, or worse. The orcs have struck Veldaren once. They may well have found a way across the bone ditch again."

"Hard to rest with torchlight flickering into your bedroom," said an elderly man behind Jeremiah.

"Something ain't right, Corren," Jeremiah said, "and I'd bet all my harvest you feel it stronger than we do."

Corren stroked his beard as his eyes went blank.

"Two men come from the east," he said, his voice distant. "But they are not men. Troubled spirits, half-demons..."

The two farmers stared at Corren in horror as the old man's voice returned to normal.

"Ashhur will not grant me to see any more."

"Gather the children on the west side of the town," Jeremiah ordered. "Tell everyone they must be ready to flee."

"Flee from what?" the farmer asked.

"It doesn't matter!" Jeremiah shouted. "Tell the others!"

The man went to do as ordered. He had not the heart to argue, not with the fear of his nightmare still lingering. He spread the word to the rest searching the town.

"Ashhur help us," Corren suddenly whispered. "Hurry. I feel they have arrived."

A warcry rolled from the east, a primal, mindless roar that shook every man in the village.

"Flee west," Jeremiah ordered Corren. "And take every one you find with you."

The old man put a hand on the young farmer's shoulder.

"Fear not," he said, a weak smile on his face. "Ashhur's golden eternity awaits us."

Jeremiah raised his sword so that the flame of his torch flickered across it.

"Not this night, not if I can help it," he said before running toward the battle cry.

The town held only ninety members, half of them younger than eighteen. When the second brutal cry rolled over the houses, most were running west, dragging children and carrying young ones in their arms. The men, young and old, took up torches, shortswords, even rakes and sickles, and prepared to defend their homes. Bravely they fought, and bravely they died.

"Run, run, run!" Jeremiah shouted to a mother pulling along a young boy. "Run west, and don't look back!" A horrible shriek of pain tore his attention past them to a circle of torches, held by the gathered defenders of the small village. He kissed his sword as he approached, horrified by the massacre he saw in the dim light.

A great half-orc bore down on a strong child of thirteen that Jeremiah knew well. Strength in fields and spirit meant little compared to the might of a warrior conducting the dark god's power. Condemnation tore through his rusted sickle, cut his arm from his body, and then hooked around, severing his ankles. The boy fell, dying in four pieces.

Jeremiah knew then he would enter the golden eternity before the dawn.

Someone swung a torch while another man thrust his short sword. The half-orc shattered the sword with a savage swipe while ignoring the torch as it smashed across his leather armor. He roared as he chopped that man's head into pieces. The dropped torch sputtered and died.

All the courage he could muster failed to move Jeremiah forward. He watched the raging warrior butcher friend after friend, so many having never seen their eighteenth winter. Harruq tore a neck open, punctured the same man three times, and then gutted another who had closed the distance. The man died after his final slash passed an inch from the half-orc's skin.

"Come on," Jeremiah said to himself. "Hang it all, come on!"

The half-orc held both swords out wide and roared at the remaining three facing him. When they held their ground, Jeremiah could bear the sight no more. He charged, screaming the cry of one expecting to die. He did not get far though, for a sharp burning pain enveloped his wrist. His arm jerked back, and the sudden force spun him to his knees. As he knelt there, a voice spat down at him.

"Pitiful."

Jeremiah looked up to see another half-orc clad in ragged robes. The fire came once more, wrapping around his throat. Smoke blurred his vision, the smell of his own charring flesh filled his nose, and he dropped his sword to claw at his neck. Flesh burned off his fingers. He felt the pain fade away. Then nothing.

The whip slithered off his throat and coiled around the half-orc's hand.

"Simply pitiful," Qurrah said again, but Jeremiah did not hear it. His soul was already on its way.

<hr>

Red eyes watched from afar, their owner relishing the carnage amid the dying torchlight. A smile grew on his ever-changing face.

"Beautiful," Velixar whispered as the number of dead grew. Shifting sighs and mindless moans drifted from behind. Velixar glanced back at his companions, who now numbered in the thousands.

"Surround the town," he commanded them. The nearest nodded, the movement swinging the entirety of his rotting face. He moaned to the others, sending them in motion. The man in black extended a hand to his two disciples.

"Send on their souls," he said, "but leave the bodies for me."

<hr>

Harruq stormed through the village, roaring for any to stand and fight.

"We're coming for you," he shouted, his voice like the growl of a dog. "You are weak! Weak!"

The cry of a child sent him bashing through the door of a small home. Inside, a girl huddled beside her much younger sister. They were wrapped in blankets. The little girl clutched a doll in her hands. Harruq paused, and deep in his heart, some piece of him shrieked in protest.

"I'm sorry," he said. Salvation and Condemnation quivered in his hands. "There's no room for compassion. Not here. Not tonight."

He left the house, blood covering his blades. He let out a primal cry to the stars, whether of anguish or elation, he did not know.

<hr>

Qurrah broke away from his brother when the last died before them. He could smell the fear of the villagers, and like a tracking dog he could use it to find where they fled.

Flames danced across the side of one house, alerting Qurrah. The half-orc coiled the whip around his arm and pulled out a scrap of bone from a pouch. It was time to test the spells his master had taught him. An elderly man came around the corner, a torch his only weapon. He glared at Qurrah with unabashed hatred.

"*Weakness*," the necromancer hissed in the wispy tongue of magic. The old man dropped his torch and wobbled on his legs. His elderly arms, already shriveled, shrunk even more. Skin tightened against his frame, and in seconds it was if the man had become a living skeleton decorated with flesh, hair, and clothes. The man took a staggered step forward, still determined to fight Qurrah even as his arms struggled to bear their own weight. He let out a moan of unintelligible loathing.

"You are not worth my time," Qurrah told him. "So consider this an honor for your determination."

He began casting, relishing the feeling of control flowing throughout his body. Never before had he felt so powerful, so invincible. He prayed the night would never end.

"*Verl Yun Kleis*," he hissed. *Hands of ice*. The half-orc lunged forward, grabbing the old man by the wrist. Blue light swirled around the contact of their flesh, causing the water and blood inside his arm to freeze. Qurrah's smile broadened as the man collapsed and died while still within his grasp. When he let go, the icy flesh hit the dirt hard enough to crack the arm at the shoulder. Blood poured out from the body but not the arm.

"A marvelous spell," the half-orc gasped, fighting away a momentary wave of dizziness.

He closed his eyes and attuned his mind to the village. A stench of fear trailed west. Women and children, all of them panicked and confused.

"Harruq, they flee west," Qurrah whispered, magically enhancing his voice using a spell Velixar had taught him. His quiet words flooded the town, audible by all yet still sounding like a whisper. The fleeing residents of the town heard and were terrified. His brother heard and obeyed.

The two met at the edge of town. They saw scattered groups of families not far in the distance.

"Get them, my brother," Qurrah ordered. "None may live or they will tell of the half-orcs who destroyed their town."

"Then they're dead," Harruq said, clanging his swords together. Power crackled through them. He took up the chase.

An elderly man and woman, propping each other up as they ran side by side, refused to turn when Harruq barreled toward them. Salvation took the woman's life, Condemnation the man's. The two bodies collapsed, their lifeless limbs entangled. Not far ahead of them, a woman ran in only her shift, a child clutched to her breast.

"Why do you flee?" Harruq roared when her crying eyes glanced back at him. "This life is pain, suffering! I'm here to end it, end it all!"

The woman ran faster and her child cried louder. It didn't matter. Harruq rammed her with his shoulder. To protect her child, the woman rolled so that her side took the brunt of the fall. As the half-orc's blades twirled in the air, the mother kissed her child one last time before curling up around the joy of her life. Then the blades fell.

On the half-orc ran. Innocent blood stained his sword as life after life ended. Harruq felt no remorse and saw no pain. The blood haze of rage and dark magic blocked all. Man, woman, child, it didn't matter. They all died. Only seven managed to keep ahead of his berserking madness: a mother, her two children, a few farmers, and their daughters. They dared to hope.

As they ran, a strange sight met their eyes. In the distance were hundreds of bodies lined in perfect formation. They held no torches or lanterns. The wind shifted, and upon its gentle flow the stench of death came to them. The villagers slowed, fearfully eyeing the line. The stars were bright, and there was no mistaking that something was amiss. They were no soldiers. Only a scattered few wore armor. Still, they stood in the straight lines of a disciplined army.

A roar from Harruq at their heels spurred them on. They charged the line, crying out for aid.

"A creature attacked our town," shouted the mother. "Please, my daughter is still there. They might hurt her. Please, help us!"

"There's two," shouted one of the farmers. "They killed my wife! You have to…"

Their words trailed off once they were close enough to see clearly. Flesh hung from their bones, pale and rotting. Wounds spotted nearly every one, although no blood poured from them. Their saviors were men, orc, and elf, but they were dead.

"Ashhur help us," an exhausted farmer murmured before the line advanced upon them. The Forest Butcher at their heels, they could not run. Velixar's army of undead tore the seven apart and cast their remains to the dirt. So ended the last life of Cornrows.

Harruq halted before the mess that had been his prey. The line of undead stood motionless, their unfocused eyes looking nowhere. The wind blew through them, shifting their hair and whistling through the holes in their bodies. The half-orc said nothing, just stared at the carnage and the servants of his master as he waited for Qurrah. The mindless rage that had consumed him slowly faded. By the time his brother arrived, it was all but a memory.

"The undead took them," Qurrah said, his breath quick and shallow. "Velixar did not trust us."

"I trust little," Velixar said, stepping through the line of his servants. "The truth is I do not take risks. If any survived you would have been identified and my plans ruined."

Both brothers bowed to their master.

"What are the plans you speak of?" Harruq asked.

"In time, my dear bone general, I will tell you both. For now though, I must deal with your brother." Velixar brought his gaze to the young necromancer.

"Let us return to the village. It is time we test your power."

The three stood in the center of the town, corpses scattered in all directions. There was an eerie silence creeping about, its soft touch tickling Harruq's spine. He held the hilts of his twin blades in his hands, drawing comfort from them. At that dark moment, it was his only comfort.

"You know what I ask of you," Velixar said.

"I do," Qurrah said. "I pray I do not disappoint."

He closed his eyes, his hands stretched to either side. His fingers hooked and curled in strange ways, many times so twisted and odd that Harruq could not bear to watch them dance. Words spilled from the frail half-orc's lips. Some were strong, demanding, while others came limping out, twisted in form and barely existing as they were meant to exist. The words, however, did not matter as much as the dark power rolling forth from Qurrah. His sheer will would determine the full strength of the spell.

A cold wind came blasting in, seemingly from all directions. Faster and faster, the words poured from Qurrah's pale lips. Harruq braced himself as his hair fluttered before his eyes. The spell neared completion, and Velixar hissed in sheer pleasure at the power flaring from his apprentice. Qurrah shrieked out one final word, the signal, the climax of the spell.

"*Rise!*"

All around corpses staggered to their feet.

"Qurrah," Harruq stammered but could say no more.

"Eight," Qurrah gasped, dropping to his knees. "It is…I am sorry, master."

Velixar walked about, examining each of the undead farmers. He remained quiet, hiding all emotion from his apprentice and even refusing to look at him.

"This is the first time you have ever brought the dead back to life," Velixar said. "Correct?"

"Of this size, yes," Qurrah answered. His entire body rose and fell according to his unsteady gasps.

The man in black turned to him.

"When I was first taught that same spell I managed only four. Rise from your feet, Qurrah Tun." He faced the undead. "Kneel!" he shouted to them. At once, the eight bowed to Qurrah. Velixar placed a hand on the half-orc's shoulder.

"It is your servants that should bow to you," he said. "And one could not ask for a more gifted disciple."

Qurrah stood but kept his head bowed. Harruq shifted on his feet, scared and confused. The eyes of his brother…tears?

"Thank you, my master," whispered the half-orc. "I have never felt more honored."

Velixar placed a hand atop Qurrah's head and accepted the tears he knew the half-orc tried to hide. He had long thought the weaker emotions fled from his soul, but that night he felt an overwhelming sense of pride.

"Harruq," Velixar said, his normally unshakable voice faltering. "Escort your brother home. Protect him, even unto death. He will usher in a new age to this world. Of this I have no doubt." He shouted an order to Qurrah's undead. The eight obeyed, marching out of town to join the rest of Velixar's army.

"I will take control now," he said to his disciple. "In time, the burden of sustaining life in them will seem weightless. Until then, let me bear it. Look at me."

Qurrah did, his eyes red and his face wet. "Yes master?" he asked. No weakness tainted his voice. The man in black put a hand on either side of Qurrah's face and drew him close.

"Become a god among men," he whispered. "Remain faithful to me, and to Karak, and I shall see it come to pass."

Qurrah nodded but said nothing. Instead, he turned and joined his brother.

"Let's go home," he said.

"I'm thinking that's a great idea," Harruq said. The two stepped around the bodies of the slain as they headed east, leaving Velixar alone in the emptiness of Cornrows.

"Incredible," Velixar said when they were gone. "Never would I have guessed they had such power." He paused, listening to the words of his master. The man in black smiled.

"If you didn't know then I do not feel as blind," he said. "He will surpass me. Surpass us all. Should I bring him to your dark paladins?"

Karak's answer was swift.

Let him learn at your side. He loves you, and this love will drive him to power not seen since I walked Dezrel. Use it. Give me a sacrifice worthy of my name. Burn the east to the ground.

Velixar closed his eyes and bowed his head in acknowledgement.

"Only in absolute emptiness is there order," he said, the goal of all those who worshiped Karak and knew the true purpose of their lives. "And I will bring order."

The Tun brothers did not go straight home that night. Harruq veered them off into the grassy hills south of Woodhaven.

"Why do we go this way?" Qurrah asked, his arm draped around his brother. His sagging body seemed ready to collapse into slumber at any time.

"I need to retrieve the swords I dropped," Harruq said quietly. "I want to train with them."

Qurrah nodded so absently that Harruq wondered if his brother even heard him. They walked in silence under the beauty of the stars.

"Hey, Qurrah?"

"Yes, brother?"

"What we did...is it..."

"Did you revel in the power granted to you?" Qurrah asked. Harruq paused, searching for an honest answer.

"Aye," he said at last. "I did."

"Then why do you now question it?"

Harruq shrugged. "Velixar's strong. What do you think he wants with us?"

"Order," Qurrah said. "We will kill, brother. It is all we are good at. It was what we were made for. What other purpose do you see for your life?"

Harruq shrugged. "I said it before. I'm here to protect you."

"Then kill those that seek to kill me," Qurrah said, a bit of his sleepiness leaving him. "Our master has given us so much. Power. Weapons. A purpose. What more could we ever ask for?"

"Yeah, what else," Harruq said, shifting more of his brother's weight onto his shoulder. Qurrah's eyes drooped, and it seemed sleep would steal him away before they reached town.

Harruq found his blades without too much trouble. He laid Qurrah down. His brother slept peacefully, and in silence the half-orc took the old weapons into his hands. He looked to the stars. Even as a child, those far away lights had awakened something in him, something so different from what he thought he was. Right then, it was awakening guilt and fear.

"I do what I choose," he argued to the stars. "No, what I *must*."

The words felt hollow, nothing more than self-serving lies. He kept remembering the mother with her young babe clutched to her breast as she fled from him. When he had rammed her, she had tucked the child to guard it from the fall. Right before the kill, she had held him, trying to protect him.

"Why?" he asked. A part of him worried he might wake his brother, but he was too drained to care. "Why did she do that? She could have run faster without the child!"

No, he knew that answer. She would not abandon her child just as he would not abandon Qurrah. Then what was bothering him so? He fell to his knees and stabbed the old weapons into the dirt. The faces of those he had killed danced before his eyes, especially the mother and her child, and the young girl holding her little sister. The fear in their eyes. The screams. The panic. Horror.

"I do what I have to do," he said again. But did the villagers have to die? All those children, mothers, sisters, fathers...nothing but a test. And all those small bodies he left for his brother to mutilate? What was it his swords were accomplishing? Every action, every kill, seemed to confirm the words of his brother. He was a killer and nothing more. His legacy would be one of death and emptiness.

The ghosts of the village clung to his back and neck. His choice was made. When he looked to the stars, he saw Aurelia's face among them. He tried not to think of what she'd say if she knew what he had done. Guilt and regret meant nothing so he choked it down. It didn't matter what he wanted. His oath was made. His swords had swung. The weight of blood was on his shoulders, and who was he to fight against it?

"I'm sorry if I'm weak," Harruq whispered to his sleeping brother. "I can't be like you. I can't be strong like you..."

The half-orc buckled the old pair of swords next to the gleaming black blades on his belt. He then gently took his brother into his arms and carried him back to town. The weight of his brother in his hands was a feather compared to the burden on his heart.

9

Harruq arrived late to his sparring match with Aurelia. His face was haggard and his eyes bloodshot.

"Rough night?" Aurelia asked. She blinked as a tingle in her head insisted that something was different about the half-orc. After a few seconds, she saw it.

"Harruq," she asked, "is it me, or did you grow thirty pounds of muscle overnight?"

"Yup," Harruq muttered. "I'm magical like that."

The elf glared at him.

"Sorry," he said, his face reddening. "I had a long night."

Aurelia nodded. She twirled the staff in the air and then hooked it underneath her arm.

"Ready to start?"

The half-orc shrugged. "Sure, why not?"

Instead of starting, she lowered her staff and crossed her arms. "Something's wrong, Harruq. Tell me what bothers you so?"

Harruq sighed and looked away. He gently tapped his swords together. "I don't know. Bored."

"Am I not a challenge?"

He made vague shrug that could be taken either way. Let her think that was it, he thought. It was a whole lot better than the truth. Aurelia, however, seemed none too pleased. She twirled her staff again.

"You might be surprised, orcyboy, but I could beat you in a spar."

Harruq scoffed. "You have no chance," he said.

"First to three hits," the elf said, taking a few steps back.

"Very well," Harruq said, drawing his swords in his gigantic arms. "Guess you need a reminder of who you're learning from." He lowered his weapons and thrust out his chest. "Here. I'll prove it. Two free hits. I'll still beat you."

Aurelia eyed him, obviously insulted. She gave him two quick raps across the chest.

"Two to zero," she said before dancing away. Harruq raised his swords and roared.

He crossed the distance between them in a heartbeat, twice as fast as he had ever moved in their previous sparring matches. Aurelia leapt backward as blades dove for her chest and abdomen. Her staff shot spun back and forth to parry thrust after thrust. Harruq pressed his attack, shifting on one foot so that his next two attacks came slashing downward for her thigh and ankle.

The staff blocked one but the other banged against her calf.

"One to two," Harruq said. He double thrust, offering the elf no reprieve. She jabbed her staff upward, pushing the two attacks high and giving her room underneath. Ducking forward, she tried to strike the half-orc's leg.

She badly underestimated Harruq's new speed though, and one blade looped around to block the attack. The other went straight down, the edge smashing hard against the top of Aurelia's skull. While it did not draw blood, the jolt of it knocked the elf to one knee and gave her a dull ache in her head.

"Have you lost your mind?" Aurelia asked as she rolled away. Harruq's mad charge was her answer, and it sparked fear in her heart.

Sword strikes assailed her impossibly fast. Any thought of the fight being practice left Aurelia's mind. It felt too real. She stayed defensive, parrying with all her skill while constantly dancing away. Harruq pressed closer, and every time the elf pulled out of a roll or landed from a leap backward, he was upon her. Notch after notch covered her staff as the swords chopped harder and harder.

His strength grew as the fight progressed. He held nothing back. He weaved his swords through three stabs, feinted a high slash, and then twirled up and around for a low thrust. Aurelia fell for the feint and brought her staff up high, leaving her lower half exposed. Her slender frame twisted. A sword cut a thin line across the green fabric of her dress but did not touch skin.

She thought Harruq might stop and claim the cut counted. He didn't.

Instead he crosscut, his left arm swiping right while the other swept left. She turned to one side, using her staff to press one sword into the dirt and knock the second swipe just above her. The staff continued twirling, positioning Harruq's hands further out of place. She used the awkwardness to gain further separation between them.

Her hands ached from the force of every block and parry. Her breath was fast and shallow. Her hair, which she had failed to tie up before the fight, hung in wild strands before her face. She was beautiful, but Harruq did not see it.

To Harruq, she was the young girl cradling her sister.

Aurelia thrust her right hand forward, her fingers spread wide and stiff. Words of power poured from her lips, and without hesitation the forest obeyed. Vines shot from the earth and wrapped around Harruq's arms and legs. Down he went. Aurelia gave him no chance to recover. She raised her outstretched hand higher. More and more vines appeared, covering the half-orc's arms and legs with green. They lifted him into the air, his boots dangling two feet above the ground.

Harruq bellowed like a bull caught in a cage. He jerked against his restraints but they held firm. Aurelia calmly walked over, raised her staff, and tapped him on the chest.

"Three," she said.

The half-orc roared his protest.

Aurelia swung the staff with all her strength. The end cracked against Harruq's cheek. Blood shot from his mouth.

"Four!" she shouted. The fierce pain appeared to knock some sense into him. He looked down at Aurelia with a mixture of anger and embarrassment.

"Sorry," he said. Blood ran from a busted lip. The skin on his cheek was already blackening.

"I don't know what just happened," she said, the quiver in her voice belying her calm speech. "But I know I don't like it and will not accept it. Ever. Is that clear?"

"Yeah," Harruq said. "Now will you let me down?"

For a moment, she said nothing, catching her breath and doing her best to calm the flood of adrenaline that still rushed through her. Harruq twisted against the vines, but they still held firm. Blood continued to trinkle down his chin.

"I'm not blind," she said, suddenly looking away. "Not stupid, either. I don't know why I'm here. Lie to me if you must, just don't expect me to believe it. Forgive me for hoping you could trust me."

The vines released, freeing the half-orc who smacked against the ground. By the time he picked himself up, the vines had pulled into the dirt.

"I have something new planned for tomorrow," she said. "Don't be late."

"You're going to pay for that," he grumbled, rubbing his sore wrists after she was gone. His heart was not in it, though. More than anything, he was embarrassed and frightened about losing control.

"It can be one of your most powerful spells," Velixar said. "It is quick, deadly, and strikes from nowhere. Listen to these words very carefully. If you give it enough of your power, nary a soul can withstand the shock and blood loss."

The man in black listed off a stream of seven words. Seven times he pronounced them, giving his disciple ample chances to hear the precise, delicate pronunciations and mimic them himself.

"Prepare the spell with these words in the morning and you may trigger it at any time with but a single word."

"And what is that?" Qurrah asked once the words were tucked firmly into his mind.

"Hemorrhage," Velixar hissed. The frail half-orc smiled, loving the sound.

Harruq sat nearby. The spidery, intangible lessons in spellcasting had little to do with him, but he politely remained silent and respected their usefulness

"Harruq Tun," Velixar said suddenly, jolting him from his drifting thoughts.

"Yes, master?" he asked, rising and straightening his back. He could feel the eyes of his brother on him and did not wish to disappoint.

"Qurrah has told me of the troubles in your heart. I must see them."

"He did?" Harruq asked, glancing at his brother. His stomach dropped, and his heart quickened as Velixar approached. He felt like a truant servant caught by his master…which perhaps he was.

"You killed many yesterday," the man in black said. "Do you feel guilt for their deaths?"

Harruq took a deep breath, analyzing every word before he opened his mouth. Velixar could surely tell if he lied. But what did he believe? Did he even know?

"I'm not strong like Qurrah," he said. "Sometimes I can be weak. Only after, though. I will try to never question the order of my master or the will of my brother."

Velixar nodded although he appeared not to listen. Instead, his eyes burrowed into Harruq's, prying information not from his mouth but from his very soul.

"Tell me, Harruq, why do you mourn the lives of those you kill?"

"I don't," Harruq said. He wasn't sure if it was lie or truth, most likely a lie.

"War is brutal. Life is brutal." Velixar put a cold hand against Harruq's face. "You do not understand, but we are bringers of peace. We will end all war. We will end all murder. We will end everything, Harruq. Kneel. I will show you."

Harruq obeyed. His insides churned as icy fingers pressed against his forehead. Images crackled through his mind. The entire world burned to ash and blew away on the wind. The painting revealed beneath was in fluid motion, an artwork of death and fire. He saw a city burning, people fleeing in the streets, and then he saw himself dressed in black armor that oozed power. Salvation and Condemnation waved high above his head, both drenched in blood. He looked like a god among men, and the way the soldiers fell at his feet made him think he might have been one.

This red-dream self looked straight at him and spoke, but Harruq could not understand the words. The sound of his own voice chilled him, though, for it was dark, it was dangerous, and it was exactly like Velixar's.

A god among men, said a second voice, one he had never heard before. It was darker than any shade that haunted his nightmares. There was only one it could be, and it was no mortal.

Protect your brother, and I will grant you a kingdom. Live as you have always lived, and I will reward you with eternity. Kill, as I desire you to kill, and you will find a peace unknown to the mortal realm. The time for questioning is over. Trust your god as I now trust you.

Love me, Harruq Tun. Kill for me.

The dream shattered. Amid the haze of red and black, he heard the cries of battle urging him on, offering him a future he had always feared and desired. A life of killing and battle. A life given to Karak. An orcish life.

The icy fingers left his forehead.

"It is a select few who have received such a gift," Velixar said in the quiet night. "You have heard the voice of the dark god himself. Now tell me, what is it you saw?"

"Please, brother," Qurrah said. "I need to know."

Harruq stared at the dirt, each breath making his shoulders heave. His mind reeled, and for reasons he did not understand, he opened his mouth and said, "That which I fear and desire. I have had no questions answered, but I do know this: the time for questions has long ended."

Velixar nodded. "Indeed, Harruq. It is time for action. I am done with both of you. Go home and rest. Tomorrow we will begin my plan. War shall come to Woodhaven."

"We await your orders," Qurrah said. The two bowed and then returned to town beneath the blanket of stars.

As the two brothers left, another soul traveled in the dark. He made not a sound as he moved. Any attempts at tracking his passage would be utterly futile, for not a single blade of grass remained bent when his foot stepped away. He was Dieredon, Scoutmaster of the Quellan elves, and few souls could match his silence, speed, or skills with blade and bow.

When the village came into view of his eagle-like eyes, his gut sank. Not a single sign of life decorated the streets or moved in the fields. He prayed to Celestia he was wrong, but his heart knew he wasn't.

He found nothing to convince him otherwise as he quickly scanned the village. He found many homes left wide open, yet none answered him when he called inside. Everywhere, staining the earth a dark crimson, there was blood.

"It is as I feared," he whispered to the night. He stood, took his bow off his shoulder, and then thoroughly searched the town. He found no trace of life barring a few rats that fed off the now unguarded remnants of food. Several homes, those with their doors smashed open, had gore smeared on their floors. One pained Dieredon's heart greatly; amid a great red circle on a wooden floor laid a small, bloodstained doll.

He said a silent prayer before moving on.

At the edge of the town, he found many frantic tracks fleeing west. He followed them, wincing as some ended in dried smears of red upon the grass. Others led far past the others. They ended at once in an enormous pool of blood, leaving the town a somber image in the distance. Chasing them the whole while were twin sets of tracks, one of enormous weight, the other light as a feather.

"Every one of them," he said, his hand clutching his bow so tight his knuckles were whiter than the moon. "They slaughtered even those that fled. Yet there are no corpses."

The corpses had been taken. Or made to walk again.

"The man with infinite faces," Dieredon concluded. Another thought came to him. "Or was it you, Qurrah Tun?"

He raced back to Woodhaven, his mind decided. It was time he had a talk with one of the brothers Tun.

Harruq arrived at the sparring point in the forest less disheveled than the previous day, and he seemed in better spirits.

"So what is your surprise for me?" he asked.

Aurelia smiled from her seat against a tree. She patted the grass beside her.

"Have a seat. How's your head?"

Harruq grumbled as he plopped down. "My head is fine."

From behind her back, Aurelia pulled out a small blue object.

"Ever seen one of these before?" she asked. The half-orc stared at it, thinking. Suddenly he knew, and he looked at Aurelia in total disbelief.

"Is that a book?"

The elf nodded. "Is it a safe assumption that you don't know how to read?"

Harruq frowned at the book. "You're not going to teach me elvish, are you?"

Aurelia gave him a playful jab to the side.

"No, it is in the gods' language, your gods anyway. Karak and Ashhur got something right having humans speak and write the same language."

"What do you mean?"

"Do you not know the story of Karak and Ashhur?" The half-orc shook his head. "I will tell you it, if you care to hear. Mankind, as well as orcs, wolf-men, hyena-men, and all the other odd races scattered about Dezrel, are less than five hundred years old. Many elves remember the arrival of the brother gods and the creation of man."

"Huh," Harruq said. "You may have to tell me the story sometime. Are you one of the elves that were there way back then?"

She gave him a wink.

"No, but my father was. I'm not *that* old, Harruq. In elven terms, I am but a child."

"How old a child?" he prodded.

"Seventy."

"*Seventy?*"

The elf laughed.

"Don't be too shocked. You have elven blood in you as well. I wouldn't be surprised if you lasted a couple hundred years yourself. This is assuming someone doesn't kill you, which I find rather unlikely."

Harruq gasped at the thought. He had always felt akin to man and orcs, whose lives burnt out so quickly. The idea of living two hundred years was...well, more than he could handle.

"Strange," he said. "Guess I have plenty of time to learn to read, don't I?"

Aurelia laughed. "You do, but I would prefer we not take too many years. Spending that much time around you is bound to give me bad habits."

She handed over the book. Harruq opened it and flipped through the pages. Each one depicted various symbols, lines, and curls. Aurelia winced at the rough way he handled the paper.

"What are these?" he asked.

"The human alphabet. And you're going to learn it."

He protested, but it was a weak protest. They went over the alphabet several times until Harruq could repeat most without thinking too hard.

"I want you to take it home with you," she said when they were done. To her annoyance, Harruq refused to accept the book.

"I really don't want to take it," he said.

"Why not?"

"Well I, just…" His face turned a mixture of gray and red. "Qurrah doesn't know I'm doing this."

Aurelia sighed and set the book down beside her.

"Why don't you tell him about me? Well? Why not?"

"I'm just embarrassed, all right," he finally muttered.

"Embarrassed? Why?"

"Qurrah's smart, can read and everything. He'd want to know why I never asked him. That and, well, you're a…you know…"

"What?"

Harruq grew redder. "An elf!"

"What's wrong with that?"

Harruq viciously plucked blades of grass. "I don't know."

Aurelia stared at Harruq for a while, her eyes probing. The half-orc endured the gaze, concentrating fully on his grass-removing project.

"I would feel better having met your brother," she said at last. "But you may take as long as you wish."

"Good. Can we spar now?"

"Of course," Aurelia said, picking up her staff.

✦

Hours later, they finished and said their goodbyes. "See you tomorrow," Harruq called, sheathing his blades. The elf did not reply as she vanished behind the trees. He stared after her for a bit, then turned toward home. Before he could take two steps, a sudden weight crashed into his side. He tumbled best he could, his shoulder absorbing much of the impact. His legs tucked underneath him and pushed, shooting him back to his feet. Out came his swords.

Standing before him was Dieredon, his bow held in both hands like a staff. Long blades stretched out from either end, tiny razor teeth lining the front. The elf twirled the bow in his hands and then charged. Two quick hits batted one of Harruq's swords out and away. A feint, so quick Harruq blocked on instinct, took care of the other. His weapons gone, the half-orc was exposed. Dieredon wasted no timesmashing the half-orc's groin. As he doubled over in pain, a snap kick smacked his chin, splattering bloodand forcing him to drop.

The sharp tip of a blade pressed against Harruq's throat before he knew what was happening.

"Move," Dieredon said. "Please, move. Give me an excuse to kill you."

Harruq was too stunned and disoriented to give him what he wanted. Instead he lied there, his nose throbbing and his swords limp in his hands.

"What do you want?" he asked, ignoring the sharp pain in his throat as a tiny drop of blood trickled down his neck.

"The entire village of Cornrows is missing," Dieredon said. "Most likely dead."

Harruq's breathing quickened. His hands tightened around the hilts of his weapons.

"I had nothing to do with it," he said. "Why would I?"

"Children have been dying since you arrived here in Woodhaven," Dieredon replied. "Butchered, intestines removed, strange carvings on the bodies, and pieces of them missing. We thought a sick mind, but now I understand better. Necromancy requires many interesting artifacts for spells. Your brother is a necromancer, isn't he?"

Harruq said nothing. He fought back his swelling anger and panic.

"I don't understand what Aurelia sees in you," Dieredon continued. "You murdered the children and gave them to your brother. You're the Forest Butcher. Admit it so I may kill you."

"I will admit no such thing," Harruq said, his jaw trembling. "You're guessing."

"I have also seen your brother meeting the strange man in black of the ever-changing face. What is his name, Harruq? What is it he offers you?"

"You're out of your mind."

The tip buried in deeper. The elf lowered his face so the fury in his eyes was all Harruq could see.

"Yes, I am out of my mind. I will let you live. Until Aurelia sees you for what you are, I will spare your life. But know I will be watching you, and I will be watching your brother. One false move and I'll kill you both. Is that clear?"

Harruq nodded, shivering as he felt the tip of the blade rubbing against the tender skin of his throat.

"Good. Pleasant days, half-orc. May Celestia watch over you…and condemn your actions to death."

The biting tip left his throat, the blades in the bow retracted, and then the elf vanished. Harruq struggled to his feet, clutching his neck as he gasped for air.

"Damn elf," he cursed. "How dare you threaten us."

His hands shook violently as his adrenaline faded. He had been terrified, convinced the elf would kill him, yet he didn't.

"Big mistake, elfie," he said. He snatched his swords and sheathed them. "I'll make you pay for that."

After a bit of debate, he decided not to tell Qurrah. Velixar had already made it clear they needed to be careful. Now he understood why. He wouldn't tell Aurelia, either. That would be stupid, and stupid he was not…most of the time.

"I need a drink," he said, turning toward the town and trudging back. All he could think about was getting a good, stiff drink. If he was lucky, he might get in a good bar fight. Nothing helped him forget his worries better than walloping a fellow drunken idiot.

10

She felt guilty for spying on him, but Aurelia was convinced she had no other choice. Over the past month, she had grown close to the half-orc Harruq Tun, and with that closeness was danger. She saw only a goofy young man while Dieredon swore she met with a killer. Only one of them could be right, but who?

Perhaps not, she wondered. Perhaps she saw the elf in Harruq while Dieredon saw the orc. The kindest man might become a brute when surrounded by other brutes. When Harruq was with his brother, or the strange man in black, how then did he behave? Could he kill? Could he murder?

She had to know. It took a simple invisibility spell to approach their rundown home unnoticed, her feet moving silently because of her natural elven grace. It was midday and the sun was high in the sky. Most of the murders occurred once darkness fell, and always when the child wandered into the forest to play. Lately no murders had been found, and Aurelia couldn't decide if she should be worried or hopeful that they had stopped at the same time she had begun training with Harruq.

Aurelia peered through a gap in the boards. She and Harruq had finished their sparring an hour before, and she expected him to be resting. She was right. What surprised her was how Qurrah remained asleep as well. Dieredon had mentioned nocturnal visits between the other brother and the man in black, but she had no idea how long they lasted. For Qurrah to still slumber they must last for several hours, if not the entire night.

She looked at him, sprawled out on a thick pile of straw, and wondered how he managed to walk, let alone cast spells as Harruq implied. His skin was pale and had a stretched look across his bones. He looked like a drained, emaciated version of his larger brother.

A good set of meals would do him wonders, Aurelia thought.

Boring as it was, Aurelia sat down and prepared to wait. She glanced around, making sure there was no chance a wandering passerby could accidentally bump into her invisible form. The sun moved along its path in the sky, and the brothers finally awoke. Qurrah vanished, returning later with meager portions of bread and tough meat. Aurelia watched, oddly amused by their silent noshing. Harruq continuously glanced over at Qurrah, and when the frailer half-orc was overtaken by a coughing fit, Harruq was there, pounding his brother's back and looking like his world was about to end. Qurrah merely looked embarrassed and pushed him away.

They clearly love each other, thought Aurelia. *Maybe Harruq more than Qurrah.*

The day passed, and it was thankfully uneventful. She was almost ready to leave when Qurrah pulled Harruq closer and began whispering. Aurelia cast a spell over her ears, heightening her already sharp hearing. A pall settled over her as she listened.

"...must resume," Qurrah was saying as her spell enacted.

"It's dangerous," Harruq said. "I thought you were learning enough from Velixar."

"Exactly," said Qurrah. "But I must practice what I learn. These nights are not enough, will never be enough. What point is sharpening your sword if you never wield it?"

Harruq had no reply. Eyes low, he stepped out into the night, Aurelia trailing not far behind. They travelled deeper into the town. A knot grew in her stomach as she noticed he had both his swords, and as they approached the poorer parts of the town, the knot only tightened. She watched the half-orc glance in through the windows of the buildings he passed. She found herself praying he only meant to steal possessions...just possessions, nothing more. *Keep the swords sheathed,* she prayed. *Sheathed and bloodless.*

He continued wandering, and she found herself circling several streets multiple times. Stalling, she thought, but it was little comfort. The day was almost done, the town covered with long shadows and darkened spaces. The older boys and girls would still be out to play, but the younger ones...

Harruq stopped. Aurelia positioned herself to the side, struggling to keep her breathing calm lest she alert him to her presence. They were beside an old house made of slanted boards shoddily nailed together. There was no glass for the window, nor a covering. She wondered what the occupants did during the winter months, preferring her mind dwell on that than the terrible look marring Harruq's face. His skin had turned ashen. His right hand stroked the hilt of his sword like an itch he couldn't ignore. He put a hand on the wood. Aurelia could only imagine what he saw: a small child slumbering in bed, positioned by the window to keep him cool. Just a child like any other the Forest Butcher had claimed.

When Dieredon had first come to her, she had expected little difficulty in the task.

"They are new to the town, and when they came so did the murders," he had said. "Meet with one of them, discover who they are. If they are the vagrant scum they appear to be, it will be easy enough to catch them in their crime. The humans can then deal their judgment with a rope."

It seemed perverse that she had met Harruq by saving him from the fate she was supposed to doom him to. Still, Aurelia was not one to judge by appearances, and what she had seen that night had seared her heart. Two soldiers beating Harruq bloody without cause or reason, Harruq who was so kind to her when they sparred, who brought her flowers and told her stories, who looked upon her like she was a goddess of light in his dreary world...

Harruq drew his sword. It shook in his hand. Aurelia watched as if in a dream. She felt magic spark on her fingertips. Under no circumstances could she watch him. She couldn't. Nor could she believe it. He was so kind to her, so kind.

"Why," she whispered.

He put a hand inside the window. The other pressed his sword against the side of the house. No longer a dream. A nightmare. She would kill him, burn his whole body to ash so she never had to look upon his dead face. Hatred burned in her breast. *Qurrah*, she thought. *You make him do this. Put the blood on your own hands, you coward.*

She knew the moment she struck with a spell her invisibility would end. She wondered how he would look at her when she killed him. Surprise? Anger? Shame? She didn't know. She didn't want to know. Magic sparked on her fingertips. Harruq might have seen if he had looked over, but his eyes stared through the window. He pulled back the sword. His hand reached in. Aurelia prepared to kill him.

"Damn it," she heard him say. "I'm sorry, Qurrah. I can't."

He sheathed the blade.

Aurelia felt her world slow and the nightmare relent. *He did no harm*, she thought. No killing. He may not be the Forest Butcher, and even if he meant to do what she feared, it didn't mean the others were him. The hope felt juvenile and ignorant but she clung to it tightly. The magic left her fingertips, and doing her best to calm her heart, she followed Harruq back home.

"Nothing?" Qurrah asked when Harruq stepped inside.

"Nothing."

It seemed Qurrah would leave it at that, but he clearly saw the apprehension on his brother's face.

"Tell me the truth," he said. "What happened?"

Harruq sighed, and he removed his swords and flung them to the ground.

"I can't do it," he said. "We don't need it. *You* don't need it. Our war is coming, Qurrah. Let us fight it when it comes, but not sooner, not now, not while they sleep…"

He looked away as if expecting to be berated for the outburst. Instead, Qurrah walked over and put a hand on his brother's shoulder.

"Be careful," he said in his raspy voice. "Your power was given at a cost. Any hesitation or doubt risks the permanency of your gift. I understand, please know that. In time, you will learn, and you will see things as I do. Until then, rest. Velixar will come for us soon. I do not want to fail him. That is all that matters. We must not fail."

Aurelia had heard enough. She knew their roles, the balance and position of their hearts. It was absurd, poor souls without a home, family, or position to be speaking of power and obligation. Her hatred of their unknown master grew. He was a puppet-master, and her dear friend was one of his puppets. If they still doubted, even for a moment, perhaps she could save them. Perhaps there was still time to pull them from the necromancer's cold fingers.

Aurelia turned and ran for the forest. Dieredon had not known of her spying, but she would tell him everything. If there was any hope, it was in his skill with blade and bow. To free the puppets, one must cut the strings.

It was time for Dieredon to slay the man in black.

That night, Velixar gave them their orders, putting in motion his plan to blanket the east in war.

"In Celed there is a male elf by the name of Ahrqur Tun'del," he told the two under the cover of stars. "He has visited King Vaelor before, and was quite vocal when the elves were expelled from his capital city. He is well known in Woodhaven, at least to those of elven blood. I need him killed and his body brought before me."

"How will we hide the body?" asked Harruq.

"Wrap it in cloth and make sure you are not seen," Velixar said. "And make no mistakes."

"We will not," Qurrah said. "How will I know where this Ahrqur lives?"

"I will show you, my disciple, but first I have a gift for my dearest bone general."

Velixar drew out his magical chest. He set it beside him and let it grow out to normal size. From within he pulled out a suit of armor stained a deep shade of black. He threw it to Harruq, who managed to catch it even though his mouth hung wide open.

"The first Horde War was caused by a disciple of mine," the man in black explained. "He blessed the armor of one of the leaders of the orcish clans. I claimed it when he fell on the battlefield."

Harruq examined the suit, turning it over in his hands. It was composed of many interwoven straps of thick leather. Obsidian buckles and clamps held the pieces together. The only color was a yellow scorpion emblazoned on the chest.

"Why the scorpion?" he asked.

"The orcs have forgotten Karak, whom they once served. They worship animals as their gods, believing they take strength from them. The warlord who wore that armor worshipped the scorpion. It is appropriate, for his opponent crushed him underneath his heel like one."

Harruq folded the armor as best he could and clutched it to his chest.

"My thanks, master," he said. "We do not deserve what you have given us."

"You will earn your gifts in time. Ahrqur is a skilled swordsman. The armor, weapons, and strength I have granted you will make you near invincible. Do not fail."

Velixar turned his attention to Qurrah.

"Give me your hand," he said, and the thin half-orc obeyed. Velixar closed his eyes and whispered a few brief words. Qurrah's head jerked suddenly, and his eyes flared open. Velixar released his hand as the half-orc murmured.

"I know where he is," he said. "It is all I can see."

"Go now," Velixar said. "The night is young. Hide his body in your home and bring it to me tomorrow. And Qurrah, remember to bring his blade with you."

The two brothers bowed and then left to do as their master commanded.

Dieredon watched the brothers travel back to Woodhaven. He had been waiting outside the town, and in the starlight the swathe of darkness rolling across the land had caught his eye. He had followed and from a distance observed the short meeting. His eyes flipped between the half-orcs and their master. His heart was torn. He had already warned Harruq that he would tolerate no strange behavior, yet he had given a similar warning to the man with the ever-changing face.

"I do this for you, Aurelia," he said, his decision made. He removed his bow and ran across the grass.

Velixar had not moved since the brothers' departure, his hands resting on the grass, palms upward. His hood fell far past his eyes, blocking nearly all of his face. Yet even with lack of sight and sound from Dieredon's approach, the man knew someone neared.

"Greetings Scoutmaster," Velixar said, his deep voice rumbling. "I would call you otherwise but I have not been granted your name."

"You have not earned it," Dieredon said. He halted directly in front of the motionless man. Less than six feet separated them.

"I have been watching you," the man in black said. "I have dipped inside your dreams. You have seen me before, haven't you?"

"You were the necromancer that led the orcs against Veldaren. You helped them cross the bone ditch."

"Correct," Velixar said, his smile visible beneath his hood. "It was a glorious day. Men of the east no longer trust the elves, and the elves hold little love for our beloved King. Of course, thousands died, but what is a little sacrifice compared to such gains?"

"They joined your army, didn't they, necromancer?" Dieredon asked. Velixar laughed.

"You are wise, elf, and you are strong, but you have sheltered arrogance."

The man in black stood, pulling the hood back from his face. His eyes shone a blinding red. His face was a pale skull covered with dead gray skin. Maggots crawled through the flesh, feasting. Dieredon delayed his attack, stunned by the horrific sight.

Velixar, however, gave no pause. From within his robe he pulled out a handful of bone fragments. A word of power sent them flying. The elf dropped low, his right leg stretching back as he crouched. The bone fragments flew over his head, faster than arrows. Then he was up, his bow in hand. The string vanished from the bow, spikes pierced the front, and out came the long blades at each side.

"You foolish mortal," Velixar said. His voice was far deeper than before, less like a man and more like a demon. "I do not fear your steel."

Pale hands shot upward, hooked in strange formations. Dieredon stabbed a long blade straight at the man's throat. The blade halted halfway there, crashing against an invisible barrier. The elf struck again, this time lower. Velixar's image rippled as if beneath water, his body protected by some unseen wall. Faster and faster Dieredon swung, whirling his blades against where he perceived the wall to be. Power rippled in the air, black and deadly.

As the elf fought against the shadow wall Velixar began another spell. Words of magic flew off his tongue in perfect pitch and pronunciation in spite of their incredible difficulty. A strong thrust from Dieredon finally shattered the invisible barrier but the explosion of power sent him flying backward. He rolled when he hit the ground, his legs tucked, and then with a kick he vaulted himself into the air. He landed on his feet and lunged at the necromancer, the blades of his bow leading.

"Be gone!" Velixar roared, the sound of a daemon unleashed. Dieredon fought, but it felt as if a thousand hands pulled him back. Pain spiked within his chest, and a sick sound filled his head as two of his ribs broke. A harrowing gasp escaped his lips. He dropped to his knees as the pressure finally ended.

Dieredon lifted the bow and reached to his quiver. The blades retracted, and in the heartbeat it took him to draw two arrows, a thin string materialized in the air, ready to be drawn. The elf fired the arrows.

Velixar laughed as they pierced into his stomach and chest. No blood ran from them.

"You must do far better than that," he said, his fingers hooked in strange positions. Another blast of dark power washed over Dieredon. He felt his right shoulder crack into fragments. Darkness swam before his eyes, darkness dominated by twin red orbs. The elf reached into a small pocket of his armor and drew out a glass vial.

"Healing potions will not aid you," Velixar mocked.

"This is no healing potion," Dieredon said. He threw the vial. It shattered. Velixar snarled as holy light of the elven goddess burned his decaying flesh. After a few seconds, the light vanished. Velixar glanced about, seeing no sign of the elf.

"No matter," he said. "Come my minions. It is time to hunt."

He spread his hands wide and let all of his power flow freely. A swirling black portal ripped into existence behind him, a bleak wind wailing from it. Out came his undead, marching in rows of ten. More than a hundred rows spilled out, surrounding their master with mindless perfection.

"Find him," he ordered as he covered his face with his hood. "He is wounded. Find him and kill him."

As one, the thousand moaned their acknowledgment. They scattered, spreading out like a ripple in a pond. In the center stood Velixar, his hands out and his eyes closed.

"Reveal yourself to any one of them and I will know it," he said, his sick face smiling. "You're no longer amusing, Scoutmaster. It is time you died."

The chorus of droning moans agreed.

"Ⅰf there was any time I needed you, Sonowin, it is now," the elf said as he fled across the grass. Each breath made his chest ache. His right arm hung limp, and his other hand clutched his shoulder. He desperately needed to bandage it but had no time.

A wave of undead moans reached his sensitive ears. Dieredon shuddered.

"How many does he command?" he asked. He crouched as he ran, his right arm dragging against the grass. Under normal circumstances, he might have been able to hold his own against the undead. However, these were not normal circumstances.

Minutes passed, long and painful. The light of Woodhaven beckoned him to his left but he dared not approach. Velixar would expect him to flee there, but he was as at home in the wild as he was in any town. He halted his run and fell to one knee. His adrenaline was still high, but deep inside he knew he had to find a place to rest. The real pain was coming.

A glance behind did little to raise his spirits. He saw at least thirty undead shambling as fast as they could in a widening arc. If he remained where he was, he would be seen.

He struggled to his feet and ran.

More minutes passed. The glow of Woodhaven drifted behind him. Breathing was agony. Moving was torment. All his extremities grew cold and his head felt light. The pain in his shoulder threatened to send him into shock. It was just waiting for his body to succumb.

His eyes searched for anything that could grant him cover. The forest was too far, and all about was shin-high grass.

"No choice," he gasped. His entire right half of his body ached. "Celestia, grant me mercy. I cannot go further."

He stumbled to the ground. His face and armor were camouflaged with greens and browns, but just grass would make it difficult to go unnoticed. Still, he had no choice but to try. He tucked his bow beneath him and then smashed his face into the dirt while sprinkling grass atop his head. He shifted his legs back and forth until as much grass sprang up around them as possible. He covered the rest of his body in his cloak. A few words of magic shifted its colors, better emulating the nearby terrain. He tucked his arms underneath him, closed his eyes, and waited for his fate.

For the longest of time, silence. His shoulder pounded with each heartbeat; his chest screamed with each breath. Colors swam across his eyes. His ears, incredibly sensitive even compared to other elves, strained for the sound of approaching dead. He heard nothing but a strange ringing inside his skull. It seemed he had put more distance between them than he first thought.

A footstep fell beside his head. His heart and lungs halted. The pain had diminished his skills. They were atop him, but he dared not move. He sent a silent prayer to Celestia as more footfalls clomped all around him. He guessed at least ten. Soft clacking sounds of bone, swinging metal, and crushed grass erased the silence of the night.

Dieredon's heart resumed. His breathing continued, slow and steady. He fought down a laugh, despite all his training. As dire as his situation seemed, he could honestly say he had been in worse shape before and survived. Three times, even.

Then his ears heard what he had feared: something walking directly behind him. The others might not see him, but seeing wouldn't be necessary if one stumbled directly atop his prone body. His good hand fingered the bow pinned beneath him. If discovered, he would die fighting. The footsteps neared. A clacking sound haunted his hearing. It rattled sporadically, and it was most certainly bone hitting bone. He imagined a loose jaw hanging by only one side, or perhaps a hand held by a thread of flesh banging against a rotted femur.

It took all his will not to scream when a great weight pressed against his shoulder. The pain that exploded throughout his body was so great he blacked out as he lay there in the grass, a horde of undead searching for his wounded form.

As Dieredon fought for his life, Harruq and Qurrah snuck through the streets of Woodhaven. They avoided the light of lamps at all costs and stopped only a moment so Harruq could don his new armor. They had to be careful, for if any saw the two half-orcs traveling amid the dark their lives would be forfeit.

When they neared Celed, Qurrah halted. He stared down a particular street for a long while before closing his eyes. Harruq waited in silence.

"That is the way," Qurrah said. "It will be the only gated home."

"I already see it," Harruq said. He pointed at a sizable mansion towering above the smaller nearby homes. The two brothers hurried into the space between the fence and the surrounding buildings.

"It seems our friend has some prominence," Qurrah said. Harruq nodded in agreement. The two-story mansion was beautifully painted and decorated. The sides of the building were a deep brown, like the trunk of an ancient tree. The roof jutted out far past the walls. It was the color of wet leaves. Many windows decorated the front, all covered with silken curtains. The fence surrounded the entire property, black iron spiked ten feet at the top.

"How do we get in?" Harruq asked. Qurrah examined the fence, his face locked in a frown.

"I don't know. I have no spells that can aid us."

The bigger half-orc stood and stretched his muscles.

"Well, up to me then." He took out Condemnation, grinning as the soft red glow lit up his face. "Let's see how strong this girl is."

He swung the blade. Qurrah closed his eyes and hoped no significant enchantments guarded the fence. If any did, they fizzled against the magic of the ancient sword. Harruq sliced two of the bars cleanly, and a third dented in enough so that a follow up chop cut it like butter. Pleased, Harruq took two of the bars into his hands. His neck bulged, his arm muscles tensed, and then the iron screeched backward. Both winced at the noise. They did not move for the next five minutes.

When both felt comfortable, Harruq shoved the third bar forward, giving them a nice clean entrance. The two brothers slipped under, the bigger half-orc having to press his arms together to squeeze through. They slunk across the lawn to the front door.

"Hold," Qurrah said softly. "I will take care of this."

Qurrah stood erect, his hands touching the sturdy oak. Words of magic slipped from his lips. The shadows that weaved about the door suddenly gained life, crawling and gliding until impenetrable darkness covered every bit of oak.

"What'd that do?" Harruq asked. His deep voice seemed like thunder in the quiet, although he did his best to speak softly.

"Follow me," Qurrah whispered. "You will see."

He took a step forward and vanished into the shadows. Harruq glanced around, swallowed, took two quick breaths, and then hopped into the door with his eyes squeezed shut. He expected to thud against wood, feel a strange sense of vertigo, or some other bizarre sensation usually accompanied with magic. Instead, he felt only the slightest tingle of cold air before his feet thumped against the floor. He opened his eyes to see a posh living room decorated with red and gold furniture, silk sheets, and a lit fireplace. Everything oozed elegance, to a point that even the half-orcs knew was over the top. When Harruq looked behind him, the darkness had left the door.

"Why did you not do that to the gate?" he asked.

"I can let us pass but a single object at a time," Qurrah whispered. "The bars had gaps between them."

Harruq gestured to the room.

"Amazing no one ever robbed this guy before," he said. Qurrah shot him a glance, his meaning clear. The half-orc shrugged, drew his swords, and began walking. A sleek staircase led to the upper floor, while through the hallway they could see a room with an iron stove and shelves for storing food.

"Which way do we go?" Harruq asked.

"Up," Qurrah said. "And quiet, before you wake him."

"Too late," said a voice from the stairs. Both turned to see Ahrqur standing at the top step, his arms crossed. He was dressed in a long green robe. Silver swirls marked the sleeves and front. Brown hair fell far past his shoulders.

"Pleased to meet you," Harruq said with a bow.

"Indeed," Qurrah said, his hand itching to retrieve his whip curled underneath his raggedy robe.

"If you are thieves, you are certainly incompetent ones," Ahrqur said, his voice full of contempt. He descended halfway down the stairs, his eyes never leaving the two. "Of course, what could one expect from Celestia's cursed?"

"We are not thieves, Ahrqur Tun'del," Qurrah said. "We are assassins." The whip writhed around his arm, begging for use.

"Arrogant ones at that," said the elf. "Such a claim is foolish. If you were assassins, you would strike without chatter. You are nothing but pretenders."

Harruq clanged his swords together, showering the ground with sparks. His armor shimmered as his anger grew.

"Pretenders with wonderful toys," the elf continued, eyeing Harruq's blades. "Toys I will take from your dead bodies."

He leapt down the stairs in a single bound. His feet hardly touched before he was vaulting over a red silk couch to land before the fireplace. He drew an ornate sword that hung over the fireplace, letting the scabbard fall to the floor. The blade gleamed in the firelight, impossibly sharp and deadly.

"I have killed a hundred like you," Ahrqur said.

"And I hope to kill a thousand just like you," Harruq said, clanging his swords together one more time before lunging across the room. Salvation and Condemnation smacked hard against Ahrqur's blade. The weapons sparked, all three of the swords imbued with powerful magic. The elf fell back, his arms lacking the strength to block the massive blow. He danced away, his sword whirling upward to deflect two quick slashes by the half-orc.

Ahrqur found no reprieve for three bones flew for his eyes and face, even veering to follow the elf's dodges. The elven blade whirled, cutting two out of the air. The third smacked into his throat. Luckily, the bone was part of a finger and lacked a sharp enough edge to cut skin. Instead, the elf was left gasping as he retreated from another series of strikes from Harruq.

"Pretenders, are we?" Qurrah asked as his fingers performed a dark weave. "How much I wish for your pride to suffer." Magical energy rippled out of him and tore across the air. The elf whirled, sensing the incoming invisible blow. Only a tiny part hit his shoulder, immediately encasing it in ice. Then Harruq was upon him, slashing recklessly.

Ahrqur batted his sword left and right, then jumped as Harruq swung back in a scissor-cut that should have shredded his waist. The elf landed atop one of his couches, balancing with ease.

"What reason do you have to kill me?" the elf asked. "Are you here for money? I could pay you twice the pittance you work for."

"Just shut up," Harruq said, hurling Salvation across the room. Ahrqur leapt again. The sword punched through the couch and embedded in the wall. The half-orc gripped Condemnation in both hands, snarling as the elf launched his own offensive series. The elven blade glided through the air, repeatedly feinting and looping wide so that Harruq's sword danced about for phantom blows. Ahrqur let out a mocking laugh, gave him an obvious feint, and then kicked high. The foot smashed the bottom of Harruq's chin, the same sore part Dieredon had hit.

Harruq staggered back, his sword swinging wildly. The elf charged in, knowing he outmatched the half-orc in speed and skill. The kill would be his.

"*Hemorrhage.*"

A sudden purging of blood vessels exploded across Ahrqur's side. The force smashed him into a decorative table. He rolled off the broken thing and glanced down at the blood soaking his robe. Despite the wound, no cut or hole was visible in the cloth.

"You are pathetic, Ahrqur," Qurrah said, his hands whirling. "You are skilled but you are soft. You lack spirit, will. It is why you cannot resist my power. *Hemorrhage!*"

A visible wave of distorted reality crossed the distance between the necromancer and Ahrqur. The elf crossed his arms against the blow. His mind was nearly overwhelmed by the sudden tearing sensation that hit him. Blood splattered from two horrid gashes along his forearms, soaking the carpet crimson. He collapsed to one knee, his hands latched around his sword. He tried to raise the blade, but all the strength had left his hands. He had lost too much blood. When Harruq came charging forward, Condemnation red and hungry, all he could do was dodge.

Condemnation shattered what remained of the table. The elf rolled, his arms tucked against his chest. When he pulled out of the roll, he dashed for a large dresser. Inside was a stash of healing potions. All he needed was one and he could fight again. Just one. As he reached to open a drawer he felt his leg jerk back, halting his momentum. He crashed to the floor, screaming in pain as one of his forearms landed hard. Then he felt his ankle start to burn.

"Take him, brother," Qurrah said, his whip wrapped around Ahrqur's left foot. Harruq did not bother to cross the distance. He had had enough. Condemnation flew through the air, its aim true. The blade sank into the elf's back. Blood and fluid covered the carpet as all life fled the body of Ahrqur Tun'del.

Harruq strolled forward, the sound of his ragged breathing filling the sudden quiet. He drew out his sword, grimacing at the sick wet sound it made.

"What do we do about all the blood?" he asked.

"We will clean it, but first we must drain the body."

The two dug through dressers upstairs, grabbing old and expensive robes and shirts. They then dragged the body outside to where the deceased elf had kept a private garden. Thick brick walls guarded against any prying eyes. They dug a large hole in a corner and then bled the body dry, letting the fluids soak into the dirt. Occasionally, they would halt and listen, worried their violent struggle had reached unwanted ears. No curious investigators arrived, however, and they continued with their dark deed. When the blood dripping from the elf's wounds became but a trickle, they filled the hole and moved on.

Using the clothes and robes from upstairs, the two brothers wiped away as much of Ahrqur's blood as they could. They tossed the bloody clothes, the table, and the pieces of glass they into the fireplace and burned them. Harruq wrapped the body in spare blankets he found in a closet.

"Grab the sword," he said as he hoisted the dead elf onto his shoulder.

"I have it," Qurrah said, retrieving the elven blade and its dark green sheath from the floor. They gave one last look around. Everything was back in place. No drawers remained open or scattered, no blood stained the floor, and only the sword that used to hang above the fireplace was blatantly missing.

"Come brother, the night is waning fast," Qurrah said.

Harruq shifted the body to a more comfortable position.

"Lead the way."

The two slipped out the front door and into the night. Upon arriving home, Harruq tossed the body into the far room, stripped off his gorgeous black armor, and plopped down onto the bed.

"Night, Qurrah," he said. "Sorry, but that elfie wore me out, and I never thought cleaning a place could be so tiring. I need to rest."

"Good night, then," Qurrah replied, crawling onto his side of the uncomfortable bed. He curled his rags about him and drifted off to sleep, pleasant memories of the battle looping in his mind.

11

Dieredon was stunned by the simple fact that he was awake. He had expected death. He had also expected darkness. Instead, the welcoming light of morning met his eyes when he leaned up and looked around. The elf smiled, then laughed. They had walked right over him but not seen him.

"Thank you, Celestia," he said, his smile remaining even as the pain in his ribs and shoulder reawakened. The stinging, however, paled compared to the previous night. He sat up, cradling his right arm. A look around showed no sign of Velixar or his undead. The morning continued to be full of delightful surprises. The elf pulled out a roll of thick cloth from a knapsack and began bandaging his wounds.

"Aurelia, we need to talk," Dieredon said while fashioning a sling for his right arm. "Those half-orcs have some very interesting friends."

He stood, tested the tightness of his bandages, took up his bow, and then headed for town.

Harruq awoke late the next morning. His tired eyes winced at the sunlight. He covered his face with an arm, moaning against the evils of interrupted sleep. Then he remembered Aurelia.

"Aaah, I'll be late," he said. He rubbed his eyes once, and then blinked when he saw his brother leaning against the far wall, waiting for him.

"What will you be late for?" Qurrah asked, his voice hinting only mild curiosity but his eyes revealing otherwise.

"Nothing. Just my practice is all."

"Indeed. Your practice. I have held my tongue, Harruq, but I will hold it no longer. Your hair is cut. You come back every morning bruised. What is it that you hide from me?"

Harruq lowered his eyes in shame. "It's not...I didn't mean anything..."

"What is it, Harruq? Tell me the truth."

"I...I've been training with someone."

Qurrah crossed his arms. "Who is he?"

The half-orc chuckled.

"She, not he. She saved my life, and she's also been teaching me to read."

"How did she save your life?" Qurrah asked.

"Remember a few months back when I came home beaten, bloody, and blue?" he asked. "Guards caught me trying to sneak inside Maggie's Tavern. They attacked me, said they were going to arrest me as the Forest Butcher. Aurelia stopped them."

Qurrah rubbed his chin, lost in thought. He glanced at Harruq, a tiny smile forming on his face.

"May I meet her?"

Harruq immediately began blubbering.

"No, but you see, I don't know if she's ready, and you might not...I need to let her know you're coming first!"

Qurrah chuckled.

"Why do you worry?"

The big half-orc let his gaze drop to the floor. "She's an elf. Is that alright?"

Qurrah walked over and put a hand on Harruq's shoulder.

"You may be with whoever you wish, my dear brother. Just do not try to deceive me."

Harruq nodded. "Alright, then you can come this morning. We've got to hurry though, or we'll be late."

"I am ready," Qurrah said. "When *you* are ready, lead on."

The big half-orc flew about their home, grabbing his old swords and donning his faded leather armor. When ready, he nodded to Qurrah, who let out a rare laugh.

"You are amusing, brother," was all he said before following him out.

"This is it," Harruq said as he gestured about the small clearing he and Aurelia sparred in.

"Where is she?" Qurrah asked. Harruq shrugged in response.

"She's never here. She always shows up after I do."

The smaller half-orc scanned the area, seeing no sign of the elf.

"Perhaps she is not coming," Qurrah offered. "You are late, after all. On the other hand, perhaps I scared her off. I do have a creepy aura about me, wouldn't you agree?"

"Suuuure, Qurrah," Harruq said, crossing his arms as he waited. "You're big and scary and send little kiddies running when they see you on the street."

"I wouldn't be surprised," said a female voice behind the two brothers. "Any man who would hang out with a brute like Harruq must be a disturbed individual."

Both turned to see Aurelia step out from behind a tree. She smiled at Harruq, and then nodded to his brother.

"Care to introduce me?"

"Oh yeah, this is--"

"Qurrah Tun, my lady," Qurrah said with a bow that sent Harruq's jaw dropping. "It is a pleasure to meet you. May I have the name of the one who has brought civility to my brother?"

Aurelia laughed at Harruq's flabbergasted look.

"I am Aurelia Thyne," she said, offering a quick curtsy. "And it will take years to civilize that big lug. I'm not sure I have the patience."

"If your patience matches your beauty then my brother will soon be dressed in nobles' finest, sipping wine and commenting on the taxing errors of our dear King of Neldar."

Aurelia blushed. She smiled at Qurrah. "You surprise me. It truly is a pleasure to meet you."

"And it is a pleasure to meet the elf that my brother is so smitten for."

Aurelia giggled at Harruq's squirming. "He's a loveable puppy dog, but I do not think he is smitten. Are you, Harruq?"

"Um, course not," the half-orc said. Aurelia and Qurrah shared a quick, knowing smile. The frail half-orc's face lost much of its lifelessness, and a gentle caring filled his eyes. His seriousness quickly buried it, but Aurelia had seen enough.

"I shall leave you two to your studies and sparring," Qurrah said after a long pause to torture Harruq. "Although I doubt the wisdom of leaving him alone with such a beautiful teacher."

"Good thing you will not have to worry about that, considering I see no beautiful teachers around," Aurelia replied.

Qurrah walked to Aurelia and bowed again, taking her hand in his and kissing it. As Aurelia smiled, he rose and whispered into her ear.

"He loves you, elf. I can feel it. Do you love him back?"

"I don't know," she whispered.

"Will you hurt him?"

"Never."

"Then accept my blessing."

Finished, Qurrah bowed once more, wished his brother good luck, and then trudged through the forest toward Woodhaven. When he was out of earshot, Aurelia walked over to Harruq and jabbed him in the side with a finger.

"Now why did you take so long to let me meet him?" she asked.

"I, but, he, but…"

"No buts. He was a perfect gentleman."

The half-orc threw his arms up in surrender. He sat down beside her and did his best to focus on the letters. Aurelia seemed impressed enough with his progress, and they soon began working on simple words further into the book.

"Why does your brother speak so strangely," she asked once they were done, trying to broach the subject casually. She sat stretched out on the grass, her legs crossed and her weight leaning back on her arms. The whole time they had taught she had found her mind wandering to the sick, spidery voice Qurrah spoke in, a voice that had nearly spoiled his otherwise surprising charm.

"Qurrah was sold to a necromancer. I told you that, right?"

Aurelia nodded. "I believe you did."

"Well, he caught my brother practicing a spell once. Qurrah was forbidden from ever casting magic, yet he tried anyway. He's like that, always been, always will. Anyway, his master took a hot poker and shoved it down his throat. Said that way he'd never cast again."

Harruq chuckled.

"He was wrong, obviously. Qurrah was stuck talking like that. Like a snake hiss or a raspy whisper."

"Or a dying man," Aurelia whispered, so soft that Harruq could not make out her words.

The streets were all the same to him, so down them all he wandered. The image of Aurelia and Harruq danced in his mind, and conflicting feelings rippled through his chest.

"She seems a kind enough elf," Qurrah said, talking to himself since he had no company. "Beautiful as well. Of course Harruq would be attracted to her. We have elven blood in our veins, do we not?"

The words felt hollow against the constant ache in his heart. Hard as he tried, he could not place it. Was it anger?

No. Surprise? A little, perhaps. Jealousy? Certainly not. Worry? Fear? Doubt?

The only emotion he was certain of was confusion. So he walked and would walk for the rest of the morning, wishing there was something he could do to banish the sick, hollow feeling in his stomach. There was nothing he knew to do though, and that made it so much worse.

◁◈▷

Their sparring ended, Harruq and Aurelia sat side-by-side against a tree, both glistening with sweat.

"Getting better," the half-orc said. "You're going to be beating my ass in a few weeks if you keep learning as fast as you are."

"Don't worry," she said, patting his hand. "Your ass is safe with me."

Harruq laughed at the absurdity. Aurelia, meanwhile, absently drew lines in the dirt. He watched for a moment, suddenly nervous and quiet. The words of his brother echoed in his head.

"Aurry?" he asked. "You said most elves remember when men were created...do you know how orcs were made?"

The elf looked at him. She was trying to read him, Harruq could tell, but he endured it without protest.

"When Ashhur and Karak warred, there were elves that sought to end it," she said. "Against Celestia's orders, they joined Karak, hoping their aid would finally end the conflict. When our goddess imprisoned the two gods, she cursed those elves. She stripped them of their beauty, their intelligence, and their long life. They weren't evil, Harruq, but Karak offered them strength and they accepted it. The dark god drove them to war against elves and men. Finally the orcs were banished to the Vile Wedge between the rivers."

"Do any still worship Karak?"

"Most don't," Aurelia said. "They've turned to worshipping animals now. I've even heard of some worshipping Celestia once more, hoping she will forgive them and remove their curse. They are a sad race, Harruq, but believe me in saying there is no shame in your blood."

The half-orc shifted uncomfortably, unable to meet Aurelia's eyes. He watched her trace lines in the grass. Seeking a way to lighten the mood, he asked her how to spell his name.

"Harruq?" she asked. "Hrm. My best guess would be H-a-r-r-u-k."

A soft blow of air from her lips turned the grass to dirt so that a large space lay available for her to write on. She wrote 'Harruk' in the dirt with her finger, spacing out each letter. Harruq stared at the words representing his name, feeling a tiny thrill.

"How about my last name, Tun?"

She wrote out T-u-n. The half-orc stared, absorbing every detail of his name.

"Can I see your name?" he asked. Aurelia nodded, tracing her hand across the dirt.

"A-u-r-e-l-i-a."

The half-orc smiled at the name.

"It even looks all pretty," he said, eliciting a laugh. "Do Qurrah now."

Aurelia did not begin writing immediately, instead thinking over the pronunciation.

"Qurrah," she said at last. "It is a little tricky, but I bet it is spelled like this."

Letter by letter she wrote 'Qurrah' in the dirt. Harruq stared at it, whispering his brother's name as his eyes traced the letters. As he did, a thought hit him. His eyes went back and forth from his own name and Qurrah's.

"You spelled my name wrong," Harruq said.

"What? How?"

The half-orc reached over, erased the k in his name and drew a clumsy, capitalized Q at the end. He leaned back and smiled. The name in the dirt now read 'HarruQ'.

"Why did you change it?" she asked. "It's a rather odd spelling."

"Look at my brother's name," he said. Aurelia did, and then she saw what Harruq had also seen.

"Your name is your brother's, only backwards."

"Yup," Harruq laughed. "Mum was always smart for an orc. Even knew how to read, if you believe that. Bet she did that on purpose."

"Yes, but why?"

Harruq shrugged. "Thought she was being clever? Who knows! but I can spell my name now!"

"Good for you," Aurelia laughed. "Now go on home, you bother me."

"Well fine then," the half-orc said, feigning insult. "I see someone's jealous I saw it before she did."

Harruq dodged the first two springs of water but the third one caught him square in the face. He was still dripping when he arrived home.

"You and her go swimming?" Qurrah asked him.

"Shut up," was all he said.

Qurrah laughed. The pit in his stomach suddenly didn't seem so awful.

"Aurelia!" Dieredon screamed to the wilderness. Birds whistled, but no elven voice spoke back.

"Aurelia!" he shouted again, wincing at the pain in his chest. After arriving in town, he had found one of his stashed healing potions and downed it. His ribs had gone from several pieces to just a single break, and his shoulder was slowly regaining strength. It would still be days before he was back to full health, days he did not have to spare.

"I'm here," Aurelia said after the third yell from Dieredon. The elf turned and smiled at her even though she winced and moved to examine his arm, which remained in a sling.

"They are nothing," he told her. "Please, you must listen to me. Stay away from the half-orcs. They aren't safe."

"Nonsense," she said. She guided a hand across his chest, feeling the break. Her hand then traveled to his shoulder, and a deep frown grew across her face.

"Who did this to you?" she asked.

"The man in black, the one continuing to train the half-orcs. I approached him last night and he nearly killed me."

"Harruq is no threat to me," Aurelia insisted. "And I have met Qurrah. He showed me nothing but kindness."

"Then it is a false kindness," Dieredon said. He paused for a moment, grabbed his chest with his healthy arm, and then looked at her again. Pain was evident in his eyes.

"That man has an army of undead. I barely managed to hide until daylight. Woodhaven is in danger, and so are you."

Aurelia stepped back, frowning.

"Are you sure it was Harruq?"

"I saw the warrior with my own eyes. I ignored them and went after the master, just as you asked." He gestured to his wounds. "You can see my reward. I could not kill him. There are very few I cannot kill, Aurelia, and I do not appreciate adding another to that list."

"I will still see him," Aurelia said. "I will be careful, but I will still see him. He needs me. I know it."

Dieredon gave a one-shoulder shrug.

"Very well. I will trust you, Aurelia."

He turned to go. Aurelia grabbed his hand and stopped him.

"Where will you go?"

The elf glanced back to her.

"War is coming. I must alert my kin. If this man and his army do attack Woodhaven, he will find the Quellan army descending upon him from the sky. Besides, I have been separated from Sonowin far too long. I miss her."

Aurelia smiled for the first time since she had seen Dieredon.

"I am surprised you have gone so long without retrieving her," Aurelia said. "She is a beautiful horse. I wish to see her when you return."

"I promise," Dieredon said. Aurelia released his hand.

"May Celestia watch over you," she said as he left.

"And she over you," Dieredon replied. Then he was gone, through the forest and back into town. There he bought a sturdy horse and began his long ride south to the Quellan forest.

"It is a beautiful blade," Harruq said, examining the elven weapon that had belonged to Ahrqur. They were killing the final hour before dark. Then they would hoist the wrapped body onto Harruq's shoulder and sneak out of town. Qurrah sat meditating in a corner while Harruq yammered to himself. The blade was in one hand, the decorative scabbard in the other.

"He was a skilled swordsman," Qurrah said. "He was also arrogant. I would expect such a blade from one like him."

Harruq shrugged. "If I didn't have my own two swords, I'd use it."

The half-orc cut the blade through the air a few times and then sheathed it. He turned the weapon over in his hands, marveling at the swimming colors of dark green and black. He paused when he found a name written in gold near the hilt.

"Tun'del," Harruq read aloud, slowly and carefully. "He even has his name on his sword."

"Did I not say he was arrogant?"

Harruq stared at the name on the scabbard, mesmerized by the beauty of the writing. He ran his fingers over it, enjoying the feeling of pure gold. When he covered the second half, he paused.

"Qurrah," Harruq said. "Look at this."

The bigger half-orc shifted the blade so that his brother could see. He kept his hand where it was. Qurrah read the name, and then glanced at his brother.

"That is our last name."

Harruq nodded.

"Aurelia showed me. T, u, n, she said. And then this sword here has our name…kind of."

Qurrah stared at the name, thinking.

"He was an elf," he said. "I guess it is possible he was our father, although I feel it more likely a coincidence. Our mother was intelligent, at least for an orc, but was she smart enough to leave us clues within our own names?"

"Well, he's dead now, so we'll never know," Harruq said, tossing the blade onto the floor. Qurrah, however, was far from dismayed. He grinned at his brother and then spoke in his hissing voice.

"Would you like to have a conversation with our dear old dad?" he asked.

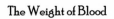

12

The body of Ahrqur Tun'del lay atop several strange markings and shapes drawn in the dirt. He remained wrapped in the blankets and sheets the two half-orcs had used to smuggle him out of his house. The wrappings provided a bit of relief against the growing smell of death that already permeated their home.

"His spirit will be bound to mine," Qurrah said, sitting on his knees before the body. His eyes were closed and his hands atop Ahrqur's head. "Any question you or I ask he must answer truthfully. Do not be disturbed by the sound he first makes. Spirits brought back into our world rarely enjoy the journey."

Harruq nodded, dressed in his black armor. They did not have much time before Velixar's dark cloud arrived. They could not rush, but nor could they dawdle. Qurrah inhaled deeply and began casting his spell.

The words of magic were similar to those when he raised the eight corpses back in Cornrows. The bigger half-orc was aware of subtle differences, but had little clue to what they were. Words of power were beyond his understanding.

The body quivered, but it was not a physical quiver. Translucent silver crept about the wraps. Blue smoke floated into the air. The blue and silver grew thicker and thicker. Qurrah's words grew louder, more powerful, and then Ahrqur's spirit ripped into the air, a glowing blue-silver form of insanity. The spirit looked much as he did in life, except his clothes were different. They were silvery robes, beautiful and decadent. The spirit wailed. It took all of Harruq's strength to resist the urge to cover his ears.

"Cease such nonsense," Qurrah ordered. The spirit immediately hushed. A bit of coherence came to his eyes, and he glared down at the half-orc.

"Greetings, Ahrqur," Qurrah said. "Remember us, the incompetent thieves?"

The spirit glared harder.

"Did his tongue die with him?" Harruq asked.

"I haven't told him he can speak yet," Qurrah responded. His eyes flicked back from Harruq to the spirit. "You may talk, spirit, but keep it quiet."

"You take my life, and now you dare keep me from eternity?" the spirit moaned. "For what reason do you torment me? I have never harmed you, never said a cursing word, but now this?"

"Just a few questions and you may return to your slumber."

Qurrah paused, a smile growing across his lips.

"Tell me, did you ever sleep with an orcish woman?"

The spirit recoiled as if struck.

"You dare ask me if I ever committed an act so disgraceful and…"

"Answer me!"

The cry from Qurrah rolled over him like a horde of stampeding horses. All his resistance broke away, meaningless, preventing nothing.

"Yes," Ahrqur said. The words dripped out of his mouth, quiet and disgusted. "Yes. Once."

Harruq shook his head, hardly able to believe it.

"You did?" he asked. "How long ago?"

"Many years. Fifteen. Twenty."

"Why did you sleep with her?" Qurrah asked.

"She filled me with drink and then tricked me," the elven spirit said. "Never would I willingly have touched one of Celestia's cursed."

Qurrah shook his head. "Answer me truthfully, you wretched spirit. Was it willing or was it not?"

The spirit gave no answer. The half-orc stood, his hands clenched into fists. He hooked them through the air as he repeated his question.

"Was it willing or not?" he demanded.

"Yes," Ahrqur whispered, grimacing as if filled with horrid pain. "When she approached me, I offered no resistance. Now will you let me return to peace?"

"Not yet. Harruq, would you like to tell him?"

Ahrqur glanced at Harruq, who was grinning wide.

"You can see we have orcish blood in us, right?" Harruq asked.

"Aye, you stink of it," the spirit said.

"Well, we also have elven blood in us. Our mum said she bedded an elf before she was thrown out of town. So guess what? I'm thinking we're the children you sired with that orc lady so many years ago."

The glow of the spirit faded. It looked back and forth, shaking and moaning.

"You cannot be bastard children of mine," Ahrqur said, his voice weak and distant. "Celestia cannot hate me so."

"Celestia has nothing to do with this," Qurrah said. "It is truth."

Almost all the spirit's glow was gone. Only hatred and disgust lingered in his eyes.

"May I be released now, wretched spawn of mine?" Ahrqur asked.

"Yes. Go rest in your shame. I have no use for you."

The spirit gave Qurrah one last glare then dissipated into the fading light. Silence filled the room.

"Well, what did you think?" asked Harruq.

"I think," Qurrah said, "that was enjoyable."

The two paused, each thinking the same thing. Finally, Harruq voiced his thoughts.

"You think Velixar knew it when he sent us to kill him?"

Qurrah stretched, letting out a small sigh as his back popped.

"Yes, I do," he said. "Although I don't know why. A test of some sort perhaps?"

"Getting tired of tests," Harruq said.

"Keep such thoughts buried and dead." Qurrah pointed to the door. The cloud of darkness waited. "Bring the body."

"**E**xcellent."

Velixar beamed at his two disciples. At his feet lay the wrapped corpse of Ahrqur. "Tun'del was a skilled swordmaster. You both have proven yourselves as strong as I believed. Unwrap the body. It is time we begin."

Much preparation later, Qurrah and Velixar stood on opposite sides of a naked Ahrqur. The elf lay on his back. Thin scars and symbols decorated his body, including a slanted Y across his forehead. Thirteen stones surrounded the corpse, each dabbed with a bit of Qurrah's blood. Velixar held a piece of Ahrqur's flesh in his right hand.

"Are you ready?" Velixar asked his disciple.

"Yes, master," Qurrah said.

The elder necromancer crushed the flesh in his grip, signaling the start of his casting. Dark, slithering words flowed from his lips, ominous in the starlight. As the minutes passed, the blood on the stones began to glow. Qurrah took up his own chant, a single phrase he was to repeat so that the spirit of Ahrqur could not flee once Velixar summoned it.

"*Drak thun, drak thaye, kaer vrek thal luen,*" he chanted. A part of him shivered, the words so similar to black words Master had spoken before the hyena-men had come. He repeated his designated phrase, feeling the magic flowing from him to encircle the body.

"*Kala mar, yund cthular!*" Velixar shrieked in a voice stronger than his frail form should have possessed. The call echoed throughout the night, sending wolves yipping away and night owls crashing in a squawking frenzy. The symbols on the body flared to a brilliant crimson.

A sense of exaltation soared through both necromancers as Ahrqur opened his eyes and snarled.

"Rise, slave," Velixar commanded. "Your soul is trapped in your body and answers only to my command."

The naked elf rose, his eyes burning with red rage. The symbols on his body faded until they were but faint scars.

"Give him his clothes," Velixar ordered his student. Qurrah fetched a pair of black pants, a red shirt, and a black cloak, all of which Velixar had prepared before the brothers had brought the bloodless body to him.

"Dress," the necromancer ordered. Ahrqur growled some inane argument, but a glare from Velixar sent him cowering.

"You must obey my every command, wretch, before you may return to the peaceful death you left. Fight me and you shall find your stay here lasting longer than your rotting body's."

The undead Ahrqur whimpered. Qurrah watched the display, fighting against feelings of jealousy. He had commanded Ahrqur's spirit to speak truthfully, but Velixar's very glare sent him groveling to his knees. The elf stood and dressed, covering his white form in the red and black garb. Once dressed, Harruq gave him the ornate elven blade.

"Your quest is a simple one," he told his slave. "Go to Veldaren. Do whatever you must to sneak into the king's castle. Kill if needed. When you find King Vaelor, wound him but do not kill him. Do not be captured, either. Die in combat."

Ahrqur nodded, his eyes seething. Velixar reached out and placed his hand on the elf's forehead. Qurrah watched as smoke rose from their contact, yet neither flinched. When the necromancer drew back his hand, a strange symbol lay overtop the faint scarring of the slanted Y. It was of a fallen man wreathed in flame.

"When you fall, the enchantment upon your forehead shall burn your body to ash. Then your soul may find peace."

"I shall do as you command," Ahrqur said in a lifeless voice.

"Of course," Velixar said. "There is no other way."

Ahrqur glanced to Qurrah, and his mouth opened to speak. Both Tun brothers felt a bit of panic, wondering what their new master might say if he learned what they had done. Instead, he closed his mouth and glared at Velixar one last time before running north on legs that would never tire.

"When will you know of his success or failure?" Qurrah asked once his eyes could no longer perceive the elf's faint outline.

"Immediately," Velixar whispered. "All he sees, I see. All he hears, I hear. His thoughts, dreams, and nightmares are available to me, hidden behind locked doors to which I now hold the key."

Again, Qurrah lusted for such power and control. Velixar smiled, clearly seeing the desire the half-orc hid behind his eyes.

"One day you will hold such control. For now, be content with what I have taught you."

Qurrah gave a soft laugh and then nodded.

"I believe that shall suffice."

Harruq did not know why, but the short exchange sent chills running to the pit of his stomach.

The night was hot and miserable when Velixar met the half-orc brothers and told them the news they had long waited to hear.

"Ahrqur was successful, and in ways beyond what I could have hoped for," he told them, joy dancing in his features. "King Vaelor has long felt inferior to the kings of his past. I have haunted his dreams, and I know his heart. He wishes a war with the elves to prove his worth. Ahrqur gave him his reason, and it was beautiful."

"What is it your slave did?" Qurrah asked.

"In a court full of human nobles, he broke through, slew four of them, and then took the king's left ear." Velixar laughed. "He killed five guards before he was slain. Two more died in the fiery consumption of his corpse."

Qurrah smiled at the image. Harruq's blood heated at the thought of battle, but the coldness in his stomach refused to succumb.

"Vaelor cannot yet risk war," Velixar continued. "He must have all the people see him as a peaceful man driven to conflict. History does not favor the warmongers, not among the peasants and scribes. They favor so-called great men, driven to war by horrid acts of others."

The man in black spat his disdain.

"It is a sad age when conquerors are seen as warmongering butchers and the cowards backed into corners are seen as the true heroes. Ashhur can be blamed for poisoning so many with such rubbish."

"What will the king do?" asked Harruq, his hands rubbing the hilts of his blades.

"He has already evicted elven blood from his kingdom. Woodhaven, however, still contains hundreds of elves. In his pride, Vaelor will demand them to leave. A messenger is already en route. I have haunted his dreams as well. He is but a distant cousin to the king, spoiled and stupid. He carries orders to the elves of Woodhaven: leave or die."

"They will never leave," Qurrah said. "They are stubborn and will defend their homes until death."

"It is more than that," Velixar said. "The Quellan elves have already been pushed across the rivers by the Mordan people. Both races of elves fear for their existence. Celestia has grown distant to her clerics. Mankind breeds like mice while the elves find themselves gradually dwindling. A man fighting an elf is like a grain of sand blowing against a stone, yet strong winds and fields of sand can reduce the sturdiest of boulders to dust."

"What are we to do?" Qurrah asked.

Velixar looked at him and smiled.

"Kill the messenger and the guards that accompany him. Vaelor will be furious at the death of family, however distant. He will have every excuse to war with the elves and we will exploit that war to our purposes."

"Will you accompany us?" Qurrah asked.

Velixar shook his head.

"Bring me the head of the messenger. I will retrieve an elf to deliver it to the king."

The man in black stood and motioned to the stars.

"Follow the left wing," he said, his finger pointing to the constellation in the stars referred to as the raven. "It will not be long before you see the light of their campfire. Make haste. The battle grows closer with every move we make."

"Yes, master," they echoed before beginning their trek.

◈

It was not long before they saw the firelight in the distance.

"Can you run, brother?" Harruq asked.

"No, I cannot. The night is long. I will hurry, but please let me rest when I must."

"Course I'll let you rest when you need it. Come on, let's go."

They stopped twice for Qurrah to catch his breath. His weak body gasped for air, sweat lining his face and neck. In the starlight, he looked so pale, so frail, that Harruq wondered how his brother could be so fearsome in combat.

When they neared the firelight, they stopped to plan.

"So what should we do?" Harruq asked.

"They are not asleep," Qurrah said. "Something keeps them awake. I fear they know of our arrival."

"Velixar?"

"I believe so. He tests us again."

Harruq patted his swords.

"So be it. What's the plan?"

Qurrah could see two men positioned on either side of the campfire. They kept their backs to the fire and sat far enough away so their eyes would not fully adjust to its light. They camped within a sparse copse of trees, the trunks not nearly thick enough to hide their approach.

"They are wise and alert," he whispered. "Perhaps I can get close enough to cast a spell on one or two. They are on flat ground, so I see no way to ambush them."

"Then why don't we just walk over, say hello, and then whack 'em?" Harruq asked.

"My dear brother," Qurrah said, "that is a very good question."

Brazenly, they approached the campfire. They kept their weapons sheathed and hidden. The closer they got before the men panicked the better.

"Halt, who goes there?" one of the guards shouted to them as they neared. They wore polished chainmail shining red in the firelight. The crest of Neldar adorned their tabards. Longswords hung from their belts.

"Me be Harruq Tun!" the half-orc said as he stepped further into the light, grinning stupidly. "And this be me brother, Qurrah!"

"Get back you smelly thing," the other guard said. Both stood to face him as other guards stirred from their blankets and bedrolls. They still wore their chainmail, proof something had disturbed them greatly. Sleeping in armor was far from comfortable.

"Me only a little smelly," Harruq slurred. "Do you have any food, me be starving, and me brother no be feelin' too good. Just look at him!"

Qurrah chuckled at the act while his concealed whip writhed about his arm.

"What is going on?" asked a whiny little voice. From the lone tent, a skinny man in purple and red emerged stinking of perfume.

"It is nothing," one of the guards said. Harruq held in a chuckle. It was obvious the guard had little love for the disgusting noble.

"Nothing? By Ashhur, it is the smelliest, dirtiest nothing I have ever seen. Shoo you foul beast, we have no need of your stench."

"You have little need of what we bring," Qurrah said, the whip uncurling from his arm and falling to the dirt. A single thought made the black leather burst into flames.

"Assassins!" a guard shouted, drawing his blade. The other guards, six in total, did the same. The perfumed man in the center shook as he realized combat was about to erupt.

"It is seven against two, you stupid pigs," he shouted. "What are you thinking?"

"That you will die last," Qurrah said before casting his first spell. The fire in the center of the camp flickered and then died. The half-orcs, through their mixed blood, could see well in the darkness. The humans had no such natural ability. Until their eyes adjusted to the moonlight, the only thing they could see was their burning red eyes, the demonic glow of Harruq's blades, and the fire that burned but did not consume Qurrah's whip. In that darkness, they were demons of another plane, furious and merciless. The men fought but their hearts were afraid. Qurrah could sense it and knew the battle was already theirs.

Harruq bellowed a battle cry, clanging his swords together for effect. The guards gathered as best they could, forming a wall in front of the noble. Harruq charged, a roar rolling out his mouth like a tornado. It was loud, strong, and seemed to shake the earth to those before it. When he crashed into the line of guards, the blood ran quick and free.

Of the seven, only two stood their ground against the glowing blades. One swung his sword in a high, round arc while the other stabbed forward, hoping to gut the half-orc because of his charge. Harruq's charge, though, was far from mindless. His speed far beyond the guard's, he knocked the stab away, then shifted his weight so that both Salvation and Condemnation blocked the other attack. The weaker blade shattered against the magic of the twin swords. One weaponless and the other horribly positioned, the two were defenseless. Salvation took a throat. Condemnation pierced rib and lung.

Harruq ripped his blade out of the guard's chest and shoved the body to the side. The dying heap of flesh collided against two other men, knocking them back and delaying their attack. He mocked them, adrenaline flooding his veins.

"Is that all you can do?" he screamed. "Where's the fun in this?"

"Here's your fun," one said, stabbing at Harruq's side from behind. The blade punctured the black armor and bit into flesh. The half-orc roared, and then twisted so fast it left the expert guard breathless. His upper body jerked left to prevent the sword from going in any further. Salvation swung around, ringing against the blade. Condemnation followed through, aimed straight for the guard's throat.

He ducked underneath the swing, feeling the air of the cut just inches above his head. Then he was up, both hands gripping his sword tightly. Harruq came charging in, both swords striking. The guard parried one after the other, constantly retreating. The others came to his aid, swinging careful, tentative blows. All three tried to engage without being put at risk, much like men prodding a bull. Of course, the result was similar. The bull got madder.

"If you're gonna fight me, fight me!" he yelled. He ignored several strikes, accepting the cuts so he could close the distance between him and his opponent. The sound of steel was quick and brutal, but after the humiliation against Dieredon, Harruq felt as if his opponent moved through sand. At the end of three seconds, both of his blades had found flesh.

The guard fell at his feet, bleeding from a severed arm and a gutted belly. Soaked in blood, Harruq turned to the remaining guards and bellowed like the mad beast he was.

The remaining two facing him were trained well. They held firm when Harruq charged, and stayed close together. Because of this, they managed to survive the initial onslaught.

><><

"**D**o not come closer," Qurrah said, cracking his whip across the grass. Fire spread before his feet, which were black with smoke. The two guards ignored his threats, knowing the difficulty of using a whip in melee combat. Casting magic would also be a great risk. They only needed to close the distance and Qurrah was theirs. However, knowing was easier than doing. Much easier.

When the two tried to close in, Qurrah lashed out with his whip. One ducked away in fear. The other managed to deflect the lash and then charge, his sword leading. The flaming leather curled back around like a living thing. Qurrah sent it at the nearest opponent. He blocked, and then realized blocking was what the whip wanted him to do. A cocoon of fiery leather enveloped his sword, pulling him closer.

The half-orc's free hand reached out. A soft blue enveloped it as he whispered words of a spell. His hand touched the chest of the guard, causing frost to spread out across the man's tunic then seep inward as the guard screamed out in horrid pain. The scream halted as quickly as it had begun. The frost had reached his lungs, encircled them, and then froze them still. The man retched silently. Qurrah ignored him, knowing he would soon be dead.

The other guard charged Qurrah and swung his longsword. The necromancer smirked, preparing another lashing. The flaming leather wrapped around the guard's sword hand, charring flesh to bone as he screamed. The blade dropped as the guard held his blackened hand before him, bits of white bone catching the moonlight.

"Mercy," he begged, falling to his knees as the necromancer approached.

"There is no such thing," Qurrah said before magically hurling two pieces of bone through the man's eyes. He turned to the other guard, who still gasped in vain for air. He watched until death claimed him.

H arruq relished the feeling of true combat against skilled opponents. One would slash out, hoping for an opening, then back away as the other guard lunged, preventing Harruq from any chance to counter. Blood ran down his arms and sides from several minor cuts. The pain was good. It helped focus his mind. It also fed his rage.

"Kill me," he shouted to one guard after another hit and fade. He smacked away a thrust but did not attempt to counter.

"Can you not kill me?" he asked, holding his swords out wide. Neither one attacked, instead holding their swords in defensive positions. Harruq shook his head, feeling his anger growing. These men did not fight with their hearts. They fought with their heads, and such foolishness could not be tolerated.

"Fine, I'll show you a real warrior," he said. His muscles tensed, his legs bulged, and then he charged the two, oblivious to his own safety. Overwhelming any of their attacks, he was a moving mountain of muscle, dangerous and powerful. The meager defenses of the guards faltered. One tried to block as Condemnation came for his head. The blade broke through and cleaved his skull in two. The other brought his sword down too late. Salvation tore through his chainmail. Harruq whirled on him, a quick double strike knocking the sword from his hand.

Helpless, the man staggered backward, clutching his wounded side. His eyes pleaded, but his mouth would dare not say the demeaning words. Harruq cut him again and again. His arms, his chest, his face: it all bled. But he remained alive, at least until that final moment when the two magic blades scissor-cut his neck. Harruq sheathed his swords and held the decapitated head of his foe high above him.

Full of pride, Qurrah watched his brother roar his victory to the night sky.

13

"**P**lease, leave me be. I can give you gold, slaves, whatever you want!"

Qurrah chuckled. "Tie the bonds tighter. I do not want him breaking my concentration."

Harruq nodded, yanking harder on the knot that held the noble's hands behind his back. He was on his knees, his silk outfit stained by grass and dirt. Blood ran from where Harruq had broken his nose.

"Name a price, name it, anything, just name it!"

Harruq glanced at Qurrah, who only chuckled louder.

"We have little need for riches, noble. All we want is you."

The man paled. "Me? What do you want me for? The elves…they sent you to attack me, didn't they? Whatever they paid you, I can double it. Triple it!"

Qurrah shook his head. "No elf hired us, and no gold was put in our pockets."

The flaming whip appeared, charring grass as it touched the ground.

"Then what do you want with me?" the man shrieked.

"You'll see," Harruq whispered into his ear before backing away.

The eyes of the nobleman grew wider, and panic gripped him entirely.

"No, no you can't. You wouldn't! Please, I beg of you, don't…"

"Enough," Qurrah said. His hand reached out, the tips of his fingers brushing the sides of the man's face. Haunting words of magic flowed from the necromancer's mouth. The noble's jaw dropped, and black veins appeared in his eyes.

"By the gods, what is that?"

Harruq followed the man's upward gaze but saw only clear night sky.

"Keep it away from me!" the man shouted as Qurrah released his hand and backed away. A glint of pleasure shone in his eyes as he watched his handiwork. The nobleman struggled against the ropes, his gaze locked on the sky.

"Please, no, take it away, I'll do anything, anything, just keep it away. Don't let it touch me, please, please, DON'T LET IT TOUCH ME!"

The man screamed for the next two minutes. Then he died.

"What did you do to him?" Harruq asked once the man was dead.

"Fear is an entertaining weapon, is it not?"

The warrior shook his head in wonder, but Qurrah said no more.

"Do we leave the bodies here?" Harruq asked.

The necromancer trotted over to the dead noble and did not answer. Instead, he ruffled through the silk robes until he found a scroll marked with the seal of the king. Qurrah ripped it to shreds and let the pieces scatter in the wind, then he turned to his brother.

"Do you remember what our Master wanted?"

Harruq unsheathed Condemnation and nodded.

"Aye, I do," he said.

When they returned to where Velixar waited, Harruq dropped the head of the noble. It rolled twice before stopping face down in the grass.

"Excellent," the man in black said. He looked his giant warrior up and down. "You are wounded. Is it serious?"

"Bah, I can handle far more than this," Harruq said. "I'll bandage them when we get home."

"Very well. Leave me. Your work is done this night."

Lying in the grass next to Velixar was the dead body of an elf male. Qurrah glanced at it, and then looked to his master.

"Do you need help bringing him back to life?" he asked. Velixar shook his head.

"Of course not. Both of you must rest. I will not be able to see you for a while, my disciples. The elves are more than wary of my presence now. Be ready come nightfall, and watch for my shadow. When it does come, that means war is on the horizon. Our glorious time has almost arrived."

Raising a pale hand, he dismissed them. Qurrah turned to leave, but Harruq lingered.

"Master," he asked, "when this fight starts, which side will we be on?"

His brother narrowed his eyes, knowing exactly why the question was asked. Velixar, however, seemed either not to know or not to care.

"If the elves win, Vaelor will have no choice but to leave them be. The assault of my orcs has weakened his army. They cannot suffer any more losses. If the humans win, however…"

A grin spread wide across his ever-changing face, chilling Harruq's spine.

"If the humans win, the elves will declare full scale war against the kingdom of Neldar. So which side do you think will have the privilege of our blades and magic?"

"We will kill the elves," Harruq said. The man in black nodded and then dismissed his bone general.

"Go. Patch your wounds."

The half-orc bowed and then joined his brother. The two journeyed across the hills and then snuck inside Woodhaven. When they reached their home, Harruq removed his armor and began wrapping strips of old cloth around his wounds. Qurrah watched him for a moment before speaking.

"You know what you must do, should it come to it," he said.

Harruq nodded, knowing exactly what he meant.

"Don't have much of a choice, do I?"

He wrapped a long piece of cloth around his chest and then struggled to make his beefy hands tie a firm knot behind his back. Qurrah crossed the room, silent. He took the bits from Harruq's hands and tied them in a double knot.

"Do your best to convince Aurelia not to fight," he said, his voice quieter than normal. "Do everything you can. Make her listen."

"I don't want to kill her," Harruq whispered.

"Will you if you must?"

The half-orc did not answer. Qurrah stepped around and stared into his brother's eyes.

"If we meet her on the field of battle, if we fight her, she might attack me instead of you. Her or me, brother. Who would you choose? Which of us will die?"

The burly half-orc buried his gaze into Qurrah's eyes. He did not flinch, and he did not lie, when he spoke.

"She would die. I would hate it forever, but she would die."

The necromancer nodded. "Never forget it. Now let me help you dress those wounds. Some look deeper than you let on."

Harruq remained silent as his brother scanned him, tightening bandages and cleaning some of the nastier cuts. His mind lingered on the fight that night, blocks he had missed, moves he made he shouldn't have, and opportunities presented he had not taken advantage of. But mostly he thought of Aurelia, giggling as vines held him and she blasted his back with springs of water.

He did not sleep well that night. It would be a long while before he did.

The mood in Woodhaven grew somber as dark rumors spread. First came word that troops were on their way to enforce an edict evicting all elves from the city. The more this rumor spread, the more elves seemed to arrive.

Elven men and women with camouflage and great longbows patrolled the city. Even more lingered in taverns and the homes of kin. Many humans left for the homes of family and friends, wanting no part of the coming conflict, while others spent hours whispering with the elf men in the bars. The tension grew. A group of men, not daring to admit where their pay came from, built sturdy palisades between the two halves of town. Everyone knew why but none spoke of it, at least outside of a whisper.

Two weeks after Harruq and Qurrah had slaughtered the messenger from Veldaren, the burning lights of an army encampment filled the fields north of Woodhaven. Soldiers of Neldar had arrived.

Antonil Copernus was quiet as he gazed at the town. The wind teased his long blond hair, never letting it rest as he stood. The moonlight cast an eerie glow on his gold-tinted armor, which was carefully polished. Behind him, the tents of his soldiers, numbering more than six hundred, lay scattered about in loose formation. In the silence, an elf walked up beside him, his keen eyes taking in the torches that lit the city.

"The city is quiet," the elf said. "They await battle."

"Let us hope it does not come to that, Dieredon. Perhaps they will accept the king's orders for now."

The elf shook his head.

"You know they will not."

Antonil glanced at the elf, who was painted in camouflage and still wore his wicked bow slung across his back. He sighed.

"You're right. I do know."

Silence followed. The two continued staring, each wishing to speak their mind but unable to summon the courage.

"You are a wise man," Dieredon said, breaking the moment. "You know who is in the right in this conflict, as do I."

"Yes, we both do," Antonil agreed. He glanced to the elf, his face asking the question he could not voice.

"No, I will not fight at their side," Dieredon answered. "Never could I raise my bladed bow against you. However, I cannot fight against my brethren. I will let fate decide tomorrow, without my involvement."

Antonil clasped the man on the shoulder. "Thank you. If there was a way I could stop this, I would."

"Then stop it."

"You know I can't."

"You can! Defy the king's orders. Stop the bloodshed that his fear and paranoia are about to unleash."

"An elf came, killed several nobles, and took the king's ear. Then his cousin is slain bearing a message to this town, his head left at the gate of our city. Paranoia it might be, but it is justified."

Antonil quieted. Dieredon watched him, amazed just how young the man could still look in the moonlight. He was a year beyond forty, yet he commanded the entire Neldaren army. Publicly, he handled the weight wonderfully, but when prying eyes were gone, his all too-human fear and doubt showed. When the man spoke again, his voice trembled.

"I will not break my oaths. His Majesty asked I enforce his edict, and so I shall."

Dieredon nodded, the sparkle in his eyes fading.

"I had hoped otherwise, but follow your oaths and your heart as you must."

The elf whistled. From the night sky came the sound of soft wing beats. Then a white, winged horse swooped down, landing in front of Dieredon.

"Come, Sonowin," the elf said to his cherished companion. "Let us leave this place while it is still in peace."

The beautiful creature neighed in agreement. Dieredon mounted Sonowin, needing no reins or saddle. Antonil saluted the elf just before his mount leapt into flight.

"Stay safe, friend," he said.

"You as well, friend."

Before the elf took to the sky, however, he paused.

"Antonil...something more is at work here. Be wary. I will not take sides in this conflict, and neither shall the Quellan elves, but if I find who caused this war, I will kill him. It is the least I can do."

A great beat of white wings and then the elf was in the air. Antonil watched him fly far south, watched until he was a tiny white dot among a blanket of stars. Before he stopped watching, however, he saw more than fifty similar white dots line the horizon. The guard captain smiled, somehow heartened by the sight.

"Let us hope for miracles," he whispered to the night. "And let us hope that at tomorrow's end all my troops are still alive."

He stared at the stars for a long while before joining his troops in slumber.

◈

Harruq and Qurrah waited anxiously at their door. They were fully armed and ready. The half-orc's sister swords were sharpened and gleaming. Wrapped around his arm, Qurrah's whip writhed hungrily. Their eyes rarely blinked, but as hour after hour passed and no blanket of shadow came to them, their patience wore thin.

"The human army is right outside the town," Harruq grumbled. "We can't wait until tomorrow night."

"Patience, brother," Qurrah said. "Just...patience."

Another hour, and still no shadow. Harruq stepped back inside and plopped down. The other half-orc remained at the door, his eyes not leaving the gray outside.

"He's not sending for us," Harruq said.

"You are correct," said Velixar's voice, startling both of them. They turned to see their master emerge from the shadows of their home, his red eyes gleaming.

"How did you get in here?" the warrior asked.

"Listen to me," Velixar said, ignoring the question. "I have little time. The elves have erected barricades near their homes. Surely you have seen them. Slip past their defenses and wait. When the battle comes, slaughter the elves from behind. You must weaken them enough so that Vaelor's army has a chance at victory."

"We will not fail," Qurrah promised. "Where will we meet you?"

"Listen for where the screams are at their worst," Velixar said as his shadow began to fade. "There shall I be."

A pale hand reached inside his robes and pulled out five glass vials. Qurrah knelt and accepted the gifts.

"The vials contain powerful healing elixirs. If either of you are injured tomorrow, drink from them and resume the slaughter anew."

"Thank you master," Harruq said, accepting three from his brother before kneeling as well.

"We will await you in the chaos," Qurrah said.

Then the man was gone, vanishing into the shadows of the room. The two glanced at each other. Harruq shrugged.

"That was easy. Bed time?"

"Sleep if you must," Qurrah said. "I will join you in a bit."

Harruq removed his armor, lay down on the bed of straw, and slept. The necromancer stepped outside his home, walked to the side, and stared at the flickering lights in the distance. Campfires and torches. An army, the same that had removed him and his brother from their home, slept so close. Every one of them contemplated their death.

Qurrah closed his eyes and inhaled the cold night air. Yes, the tension was delectable. The quiet moments before battle were a rare thing that so very few were lucky enough to experience. Fear, worry, hope, prayer, regret, and sorrow all floated to the stars.

The half-orc let his attuned mind drink it all in. Beautiful, he thought. Absolutely beautiful.

The next morning Harruq did not put on his armor or prepare his blades.

"I have to see Aurelia," he told his brother, who nodded in understanding.

"I will wait for you," Qurrah said. "Return before the battle starts."

"I will," Harruq said. Then he was gone, rushing down the streets of Woodhaven toward the calm forest that nestled about it.

◈

"Aurry, are you there?" he shouted. He had hoped the elf would be waiting for him, but as he neared their usual clearing there was no sign of her. His heart skipped, and he feared she had already gone off to prepare for battle.

"Aurelia, come on out now," he shouted again. His eyes searched the forest.

"I'm here," Aurelia said. Her voice was quiet, subdued. Harruq turned and tried to smile.

"There you are. Are you doing alright?"

The elf shrugged. Her hands hugged her sides, her walnut eyes filled with worry.

"The elves are going to fight today, Harruq. I'm sure you've heard why."

"Are you going to join them?" he asked.

The elf nodded.

"They are my family. This is my home. I cannot abandon them."

Harruq's heart skipped, and the words of his brother echoed in his head. He had to make her understand.

"Aurry, I'm asking you, please don't fight. You aren't needed. The elves will win, right? Right?"

Aurelia shrugged. "We're outnumbered four to one. We might win, but we'll still suffer many deaths. If I am needed, I will fight."

"No," Harruq said, running up and grabbing her arms. "No, you must understand, you can't fight. You can't!"

161

"Why?" she asked as tears formed in her eyes.

"I can't lose you, Aurelia. Please don't fight. For me, will you not?"

It seemed all the forest paused, listening for the answer.

"Harruq, I love you. But I also love my home. I love my brethren."

She stood on her toes and gave him a quick, soft kiss on his lips. A tear ran down Harruq's cheek as he stood in shock. His mind relished the soft feel of her lips on his, the scent of flowers, and the subtle fire that had escaped onto his tongue.

"I'll see you tomorrow," she said, taking a hesitant step toward the trees.

"Sure thing," Harruq said, rubbing the tear off his cheek and pretending it had not been there. Aurelia smiled. Tears were on her cheeks as well, but she left them alone.

"Bye-bye, Harruq."

"Bye-bye, Aurelia."

Then she was gone. He stood there, not moving, his mind a chaos of fear, swords, Velixar, his brother, and that lingering kiss. Then he screamed to the sky, one long, primal roar of hopeless confusion.

He stormed back to Qurrah, his chest a boiling pot of rage. She had not listened. He had begged, he had opened his heart, and she had not listened. So fine then. If he saw her, well then…then…

Even in his anger, he could not voice the words in his mind, but the feeling was there. Death. If he met her, there would be death, and that death would be preferable to the torment of pain he felt in his heart. Qurrah did not have to ask what her answer was when he returned to their home.

"I am sorry," was all he said before handing Harruq his weapons. "Get ready. When the fighting begins you will forget all about her."

"Unless I see her," he said. Qurrah chose not to respond. Suited and ready for battle, the Tun brothers left their home in Woodhaven for the last time.

14

"The men are ready, milord," Sergan said. "Do we march?"

Antonil stared at the small town, seeing very little motion within. No people wandered the streets. No traveling merchants hawked their wares. He sighed and turned to Sergan, his trusted advisor in war. The man was old, scarred, and had dirty hair falling down to his shoulders. He had seen many wars, and the axe against his shoulder had claimed more than a few lives.

"Yes, let us end this, one way or the other," Antonil said. "Order them to march. I'll lead us in."

"Yes, milord."

Sergan turned and started barking orders, all his calm and politeness vanishing. The guard captain glanced at the edict from the king he carried in his hand. A rash impulse filled him, an insane desire to tear the paper to shreds and return to his liege bearing a lie on his lips. Under normal circumstances the king would know no difference. His advisors, however, were many, and every one of them would betray Antonil for the chance to gain esteem in the eyes of the king.

No, he would have to deliver the message, regardless of his desires. He sighed one final time, turned toward his army, and began the march.

❦

Where Celed and Singhelm met there was a small clearing. No buildings or monuments marked it, just a single circle of grass upon which no house would ever be built. On that spot, Singhelm the Strong and Ceredon Sinistel, leaders of Neldar's troops and the Erzen elves, respectively, had made a pact that a city could exist between the two races without bloodshed. Singhelm had long since passed away, while Ceredon remained, two hundred years older, as the leader of the elven elite ekreissar.

It was in that clearing Antonil halted his army. The men shuffled around nervously, their eyes searching for enemies that always seemed to be hiding beyond their vision. The guard captain unrolled the edict, his gut sinking as he realized where he stood. Long ago, man and elf had agreed to live together in peace. Now, on that very same spot, he would rescind that agreement.

Beyond the clearing loomed several palisades. All nearby windows were closed, and several boarded. A few humans stuck their heads out their doors to glimpse the armored men trampling through their city. Most kept themselves far from danger.

"Elves and men of the city of Woodhaven," Antonil shouted. "By order of the noble and sovereign King of Neldar, all elven kind has been banned from human lands. The elves of Woodhaven have ignored this edict, ignored the laws of the great kingdom in which they live. This will not be tolerated any longer. All elves must leave the city, which being outside the forest of Erze, falls inside our borders. Those who do not immediately leave will be forced out at the edge of a sword. These are the words of our great King Vaelor, and may they be never forgotten."

Antonil rolled up the scroll in silence. Only coughs and the shifting sounds of uncomfortable armor filled the air. Seconds passed, slow and crawling.

"If one may speak for the elves of the city, please let him come forth," the guard captain shouted. "I seek the answer of the elven kind. I do not want blood spilled this day."

A single elf approached. He was dressed in a long green cloak, silvery armor, and he bore his bow openly. Antonil could barely make out his features, since he was so far down the street. The elf halted, drew an arrow, and fired it into the air. It smacked the dirt an inch from

Antonil's foot. Sergan shook his head and stared in wonder at his commander. The man had not flinched.

"I shall take that as your answer," Antonil shouted to the town. "Woodhaven desires death."

He drew his sword and spoke softly.

"So be it."

Elves appeared in the windows of every building that lined the center. Full quivers hung from their backs. Sixty more elves joined their lone companion on the street and readied their bows. The men in the center raised their shields, but they knew the deadly aim of a trained elf. They were about to be massacred.

"Stand firm!" Antonil ordered, raising his own shield. "Stand firm. Do not break formation!" A shout came from the elven side, and then the hail began. More than a hundred arrows rained down on the army, each deathly precise in its aim.

Not one hit flesh.

Antonil lowered his shield. Something was wrong. He did not hear the screams of pain, the thudding of arrows onto shields, and the angry cries that should have followed. Instead, he heard a stunned silence. As his shield lowered, his eyes took in a shocking sight. A black wall encircled them, translucent at times, but flaring when an arrow struck it. The projectiles snapped and broke as if hitting stone. The guard captain looked around, seeing his entire army protected.

"Sergan!" he cried.

"Yes my lord?" the old man asked.

"Do we have any mages with us?" Antonil asked. Sergan shook his head, flinching as an arrow aimed straight for his eye bounced away, its shaft broken. The guard captain nodded, raised high his sword, and then turned to his army.

"Stay calm, and do not move from where you stand!" he shouted. The men quieted and listened to their commander. "I do not know what blessing we have received, but when it ends…"

His voice drifted off. Movement behind his army caught his eye. He shoved a few men aside, tore through the center of his army, and then emerged at the back.

Far down the street, his robe flowing in a nonexistent wind, walked a pale man dressed in black. His low hood covered all but the chin of his face. His gait was slow and steady. He kept one hand outstretched, and from it flowed a black river that branched out to form the shield that had kept the men alive. No arrows fired. The battle was at a standstill, all because of this mysterious stranger who walked so calmly down the street.

"Men of Neldar!" this man screamed, sounding like a giant among mortal humans. "Some of you are meant to die this day. Rejoice, for your souls will leave this mortal coil in the glory of combat. Raise high your swords, and slay the elves that seek your death. Fight without pain, and slaughter without mercy. I have given them fear, and the battle is yours for the taking!"

The shield shook, power flared throughout, and then it exploded outward. The wooden shutters on the buildings shattered into splinters. The sides of homes rocked as if hit by the winds of a hurricane. Bows cracked and broke in the hands of their masters. The few stray animals hit by the wave vomited their intestines and died. The elves that endured it found their minds a chaos of horrors, inescapable terror clutching their hearts.

"*Kill them all!*" the man in black screamed. The men charged, driven by madness they had never felt before.

"Come, the battle is ours," Sergan shouted, pulling against Antonil's arm. The guard captain resisted the urge, his eyes locked on their supposed savior.

"You are him," Antonil whispered. "The man Dieredon spoke of."

"Come, Antonil Copernus," the old veteran screamed, pulling harder. "Your men need you! The bloodshed has begun!"

Antonil's gaze broke. He ran to where the sixty elves that had lined the street engaged a large portion of his army. They had discarded their bows and drawn swords, wielding them with a precision his men would be blessed to ever match. They didn't need to, for they had numbers, momentum, and morale. When Antonil shoved to the front line, they also had leadership. The sixty dwindled to forty before fleeing.

"Give chase," Antonil shouted. "Those in the back, flush them out of the houses."

Velixar watched the Neldaren army scatter, some chasing elves down streets, others barging into locked homes. Screams of pain and dying, although just few and random, filled the air. He drank it in and smiled.

"Where are you my disciples?" he asked. "Let me hear the screams of your victims so that I may find you."

Flying overhead, Dieredon watched the beginning of the battle with a sickness in his stomach. The man in black had come. He watched the arrows bounce off the magical shield, and then watched the human army charge and overwhelm the small elven force that had come to face them.

"I will keep my word, Antonil," he said. "Fly back to the others, Sonowin, we will battle this day." The horse snorted, making Dieredon laugh. "No, I am sure you won't be hurt." Sonowin banked, giving the elf one last view of the battle before soaring east to where the rest of the Quellan elves waited atop their magnificent pegasi. His horse neighed a quick question, one Dieredon wished he could laugh at.

"Everyone can be killed," he said, tying his hair behind his head. "And no, I have no plans of breaking my ribs again."

The horse made an interesting little noise, one Dieredon had long ago learned was laughter. He smacked her rump, earning himself an angry neigh.

"Fly on. You don't want to miss the fun, do you?"

A snort was his answer, but the creature did fly faster toward the rest of its kin.

"**W**hen should we attack?" Harruq asked. His twin swords itched in his hands. Qurrah, sitting next to him in a little back alley next to Ahrqur's old home, laughed.

"So eager to kill, brother? I was beginning to think you had grown soft."

The bigger half-orc smashed his swords together, focusing on the pain the shower of sparks caused his hands.

"I'm still who I've always been," he said. "You'll see."

Qurrah's smile faded at the ferocity in his brother's words. He glanced down, his mind spinning and reeling.

"Tell me if you love her," Qurrah suddenly ordered. Harruq glanced at him, his eyes burning fire.

"Why now, why do you have to ask?"

"Answer me, brother. Now."

"No. I don't love her. Is that what you want to hear?"

The other half-orc tightened the grip on his whip. "Forget what I want. If you do not love her, then kill her. Now get your head beyond her and focus on the task at hand. I want you fighting for a reason, not just to forget. Do you understand me?"

"Yeah, I do," Harruq said. "So when do we know when to start?"

Kill them all!

Both shot to their feet as Velixar's bellowing command rolled over the town.

"Which way do we go?" Harruq asked.

"Follow me," Qurrah said. The two rushed past the elaborate elven homes toward the sound of combat. They kept to the back alleys, and because of this, they met their first target: three elves fleeing toward them, hoping to use the lesser-known pathways to avoid the overwhelming numbers of their opponent.

"Bring them down," the necromancer said.

"With pleasure," Harruq said. He raised his blades and charged.

The closest elf realized the half-orc was an enemy and cried warning before rushing ahead, his longsword ready.

"Come on, pansy-boy," the half-orc warrior roared. The two collided in a brutal exchange of steel. The elf shoved his sword upward, using his forward momentum to slam the point straight at Harruq's throat. Harruq swung Condemnation left, deflecting the incoming thrust. His other blade stabbed, tearing away the soft flesh beneath his attacker's ribcage.

The elf leapt back, landed shakily, and then lunged once more. His speed was not what it should have been, though, and Harruq needed little opening. He swung both swords, the entirety of his might behind them. The elf blocked. His sword was elven-make and had been wielded in his hands for two hundred years. Never would he have guessed Harruq's were older by three centuries. Never would he have guessed that those two blades would shatter his own, pass through the explosion of steel, sever his spine, and cleave his body in two.

The half-orc continued his charge, engaging the two elves behind. They struck as one, their swords aiming for vitals high and low. Harruq knew he could not block both, so he accepted a thrust curving to the side of his armor, grinning darkly. As the sword punched through the enchanted leather, the half-orc cut his adversary's throat, using that same swing to parry the other attack away.

The remaining elf swore as his eyes grew red and watery. He backed away from the half-orc, his sword held defensively before him.

"What demon magic is this?" he asked.

"Mine," said Qurrah.

And then blood poured out from the face of the lone elf. The eyeballs hit the ground before the dead body did.

"Hurry," the necromancer said. "This is but a taste of what we must do."

"Very well," Harruq said. He tried to follow but the pain in his side stopped him. He clutched his bleeding side and breathed deeply. His armor had saved him, but the elf had managed to penetrate deeper than he thought.

"Are you fine, Harruq?" Qurrah asked, glancing back and halting his walk.

"I'm coming," he said, marching after his brother. He hid his pain well.

The alley opened up to the main street, running south from the center of town into the forest beyond. It was there that the bulk of combat had spread. Elves battled in the street, horribly outnumbered. They were skilled, though, and a steady stream of arrows from homes continued to weaken the human forces.

"Halt here," Qurrah said. To their right was a two-story elven home. Three bowmen fired from the windows at a party of fifteen soldiers. The men of Neldar had their shields raised high, but the synergy between the elves in the home and the elves on the street was superb. The Tun brothers watched the sword wielders on the ground dance in, make a few precise swings to change the positioning of the shields, and then dart away. Arrows quickly followed these maneuvers, biting into exposed flesh.

Qurrah motioned to the building housing the archers.

"Go inside. I will distract them."

"You sure?"

"Yes, now go!"

Harruq kicked open the barricaded door and then barged up the stairs.

Qurrah withdrew a few pieces of bone from a pouch. He tightened his grip about them, whispering a few words of magic as he did. Then he looked to the window. He could barely see a bow and part of a hand. Qurrah waited. The Neldaren warriors charged, hoping to overwhelm their opponents before arrows took them all. The elf in the window leaned out to unleash a killing strike, but it was Qurrah who did the killing. Four pieces of bone leapt from his hand. They hit the elf's neck and temple, making a satisfying crack.

The archer spilled through the window and landed with a clattering thud.

"The rest are yours, brother," he whispered.

Inside felt like a modest rendition of Ahrqur's home. Stairs in the center led to the upper floor. Harruq charged up them, making no attempt at silence. Either they would hear him through the chaos of battle or they would not.

It turned out they did. An arrow flew across the room and pierced his shoulder when he reached the second floor. He bellowed, letting the pain spark his rage. One archer continued to fire out the window, believing his companion capable of finishing a single warrior. He believed wrong.

The elf fired only one more shot before Harruq crossed the room. The arrow lodged into Harruq's side, and then Salvation tore through his bow and into flesh. A kick sent the remains tumbling out the window. The other archer pulled back and fired at point blank range. Harruq roared as he felt a sharp pain bite into his neck. His mind blanked. He dropped his swords. His hands closed about something soft. By the time his rage calmed, blood was on his hands and the remains of an elf lay in the dirt below the window.

"Stupid elfie," he said, gingerly touching the arrow in his neck. Not knowing what else to do, he closed his hand about the shaft and pulled.

A minute later, still lying in agonizing pain, the half-orc managed to pry open one of his healing potions. He gulped the swirling blue-silver contents and then tossed the vial. Ripping the other arrow out of his side, he felt a warm, soothing sensation fill his body.

"Are you alright?" he heard a raspy voice ask from atop the stairs.

"Yeah, I'm fine. Just had to take care of something here."

He trudged down the stairs to where Qurrah waited.

"How many did you kill?" the necromancer asked.

"Just two," he replied. His skeptical brother raised an eyebrow.

"That is a lot of blood for just two."

Harruq ignored him. "Where to?" he asked instead.

Qurrah glanced outside the door. "The battle is moving on. Follow me."

"Lead on," he said, trudging after his brother into the daylight chaos.

✖

Out the window Aurelia stared, frowning as she watched the battle unfold.

"Aurelia," called a voice from behind. She turned to see a female elf, a friend of hers from many years before she moved to Woodhaven.

"Yes, Felewen?"

Felewen stood beside her and faced the window. Her hair was tied in a long, black ponytail, her slender figure covered by rare chainmail crafted of the hardest metals known to the intelligent races. She had come from deep within Nellassar, the thriving capital of the Dezren elves, as just one of many that had arrived to protect the town.

"Many are dying," Felewen said. "The humans have a spellcaster of their own who repelled our ambush."

Aurelia nodded. She knew something had gone wrong; otherwise, the battle would have been over in seconds.

"Very well," Aurelia said. "Will you accompany me?"

Felewen smiled at her. She drew her longsword and saluted.

"But of course, Lady Thyne," she said with none-too-subtle sarcasm. Aurelia tried to return a smile. She failed.

"Come. Let's end this now."

The two left the building and joined the fighting on the streets. It did not take long before a group of soldiers spotted them.

"Show them no mercy, Aurelia," Felewen said, her warm voice turning cold.

"They will die with little suffering," the sorceress responded. "It's the most I can give."

Electricity arced between her hands. Blue fire surrounded her eyes. The five human soldiers raised their shields and charged as a single unit. Felewen stood next to Aurelia, her sword high and her armor gleaming. She kept the blade out and pointed at the center soldier. When the bolt of lightning came shrieking out from Aurelia's hands, that same soldier found himself lifted from the ground, his hands flailing, his useless sword and shield falling.

The blue electricity entered through a second soldier's body through his right eye. He died instantly. Then the remaining three were upon the elves, and it was Felewen's turn to kill. The first soldier to swing at her found his sword cut from his body, his hand still clutching it as it flew through the air. He cowered back, pulling his bleeding arm behind his shield. Another leapt forward to defend him. A longsword punched through his throat before he even saw her swing.

Shock and panic took over, and then the wounded soldier turned to flee. The final human soldier smashed his shield forward, preventing Felewen from chasing. The slender fighter flipped backward, clutching her sword in both hands. She landed softly behind the sorceress.

"Take him," she said. A bolt of lightning hit his shield, numbing his arm and knocking him back. The shield slumped low, but he charged anyway, fully willing to die fighting.

"For Neldar," he cried, thrusting at Aurelia's chest. Felewen was there first. All it took was three cuts. The first took the man's sword from his hand. The second took his arm from his body. The third took his life. A final bolt of lightning shot down the street, killing the wounded soldier who had fled.

Felewen wiped the blood from her blade and sheathed it. She used the same cloth to clean the blood from her face.

"Come," she said. "We must go north where we are needed most."

The two ran through the town, listening for sounds of battle. The worst seemed to be about the middle of Celed and steadily working its way south. They encountered a few soldiers as they hurried there. All died before they had the chance to swing their blades.

"At last!" Felewen cried, staring out from a side alley. They were behind a group of ten soldiers battling a pair of elven warriors who stood back to back. "Make haste, they need us!"

Felewen charged, desperate to arrive before her brethren were overwhelmed. Aurelia stepped into the street and summoned her magic. Frost surrounded her hands, and a thin sheet of ice spread beneath the human soldiers. Many of them stumbled, unable to balance the sword and shield in their hands and the heavy chainmail on their bodies. Felewen slid on one leg, her sword out and ready. She passed right between two men, slicing out heels and tendons as she flew by. The elf reached the end of the ice, turned, and went sliding back.

The two she had cut were on the ground, unable to stand after such precise hits. As she reached them, she stabbed one of their legs to halt her momentum, yanked her sword free, and then rolled around to stab the other in the throat. Another roll back, and she delivered the first soldier the same fate.

The elves they saved wasted no time recovering. They both pressed forward, unafraid of fighting on the ice. Their light armor made balancing an easy task while their human counterparts were doing all they could to swing and stand at the same time. Two men fell to each of their blades, bringing the total down to four.

As Felewen lay upon the ice, a soldier stabbed down at her. She spun on her rear, her sword out in an arc. After knocking him off his feet, Felewen snapped her legs high above her, spinning her body off the ground. She landed on her stomach, her sword skewering the guard's innards.

She pulled herself to her feet with the hilt of her sword, twisted the blade, and then finished him.

The remaining soldiers turned to flee, but there was one slight problem. An enormous ball of fire erupted at their feet, engulfing all three in flame. Two died from the horrible burns. A third slumped and whimpered in pain. Aurelia walked over to him and knelt on one knee. She placed a hand on his head and looked over his wounds while he glared up at her.

"Your wounds are beyond saving," she said softly. "I'm sorry."

She ended his pain with a small lance of ice through his forehead.

"Thank you for your aid," one of the elves said. "We must fall back to the forest. If they chase us there, it will be suicide."

"We will not have to fall back so far," Felewen disagreed. "They have scattered about our town. Their numbers mean nothing now. Besides," she grinned, "we have Aurelia Thyne."

Both bowed politely.

"Never could we have used a mage's power more than now," one said. Aurelia blushed and waved him off.

"Please we must…"

A cold chill spread through her body, like water from an underground stream meeting a creek. She whirled and stared down the street. Walking without escort was a lone man shrouded in black robes. The cowl of his cloak hid much of his face.

"Come, brother," one of the elves said. "It is the one who protected them from our arrows."

The other nodded, took up his sword, and charged. His brother was not far behind. Felewen joined them, for she too had watched as the black shield had knocked aside their arrows and then shattered their bows.

Aurelia did not move. Her eyes were frozen on this strange man. Power rolled off him. He was strong, and even more so, he was terrifying. She had no doubt of this man's identity; he was the nameless necromancer, one of the few who could best Scoutmaster Dieredon in combat.

"Stop, you cannot defeat him," she shouted. None listened. "Felewen, please!"

Felewen glanced back to her, and that small pause saved her life.

The man in black had made no threatening move as the other two charged. They were almost upon him when he cast aside his hood to reveal his ever-changing face, his deep red eyes, and his horrible smile. His hands lunged forward, the floodgates opened, and all his power came rushing forth. A wall of black magic rolled like a tidal wave conjured from his fingertips. The elven brothers tumbled through and vanished. Felewen leapt back when she saw the attack coming. She rolled behind a house and tucked her head.

The wave continued down the street, straight for Aurelia.

"I do not fear you," she hissed through clenched teeth. A wall of water swirled about her, flowing from the otherwise dry dirt street. She sent it forward, just as tall and high as Velixar's. The two met in a thunderous roar, intermixing in a maelstrom of darkness, water, and air. Then they both dissolved, their magic spent.

Aurelia held back tears. Velixar's magic had peeled the flesh from the elves' bodies. Blood leaked through muscle and tendon, and their innards spilled from their abdomens. She hoped they died instantly, but she knew better. They had suffered tremendously.

"You monster," she shouted. "What meaning does this battle hold to you?"

"Everything," Velixar shouted, hurling a flaming ball of fire from each hand. "I desire panic and bloodshed all across the east!"

Aurelia summoned a magical shield about her body. The fireballs thudded three feet from her body and detonated. The two nearest buildings crumpled, their walls and roofs blown back by the power. The elf winced, nearly knocked to her knees by the force.

"What madness gives you such a desire?" she asked, sending forth the strongest spells she knew. Several lances of ice flew down the street, followed by a ball of magma. The ball rolled behind the lances, covering the ground in flame. Velixar laughed.

A wave of his hand created a similar shield as Aurelia's, but instead of keeping it close to his body, he shoved it forward. The lances shattered into shards when slammed against it. The ball of magma halted when touching the barrier and then reversed direction. The elf glared, detonating the attack with a thought. Molten rock covered the street, splattering across both Velixar's and Aurelia's shields before sliding to the dirt.

"How long can you keep this up?" the necromancer asked. He took out a bag of bones and scattered more than thirty pieces. "How long before you break?"

One by one, the bone pieces shot straight at Aurelia.

The elf dropped to one knee, words of magic streaming out her mouth as fast as she could speak them. Her magical shield could halt attacks of pure magical essence, such as the conjured fire, but animated objects were a different matter. The magic projecting them would die at her shield but the pieces would retain their momentum.

The dirt before her rumbled, cracked, and then ascended in a great physical wall. On the other side, pieces of bone thumped against it, one after another.

"Cute," Velixar said, "but pointless."

An invisible blast of pure force shattered the wall. Aurelia crossed her arms before her face as chunks of earth slammed into her slender form. She rolled with the blows, her mouth casting before she halted. Ice spread from house to house, walling Velixar off on the other side.

"From dirt to ice?" Velixar asked. "The end is just the same!"

The center of the wall exploded inward, but this time Aurelia was prepared. A rolling thunder of sound shoved all the broken shards forward, sending even the remaining chunks of the wall down the street in a chaotic assault. Velixar grinned. Clever girl.

The wave of sound and ice slammed his body. He flew backward, ice tearing his skin, but no blood came forth from those wounds. The larger pieces smashed his body from side to side, which turned limply with each blow. When the wave passed, Aurelia leaned on one knee, gasping for air as she stared at the man in black, now a crumpled mess of robes in the center of the street. The body suddenly convulsed, the chest heaving in quick, jerky spasms. When the sound reached her, Aurelia knew her doom. Velixar was laughing.

He stood, brushed off pieces of ice clinging to his robes, and then glared at her from afar.

"Not good enough," he said.

Wild anger contorted his face. Black lightning thicker than a man's arm tore down the street. Aurelia gasped as all her power flowed into her shield. The collision sent her flying, her magical barrier shattered into nothingness. The lightning continued, swirling about her body. Every nerve in her body shrieked with pain. She landed hard, unable to brace for the fall. The air blasted out of her lungs, and for one agonizing second they refused to draw in another breath. Slowly the black magic seeped out of her, the pain faded, and then she sucked the dusty air into her lungs.

"You are a powerful sorceress," Velixar said, his anger gone as quickly as it had arrived. "But I have fought the founders of the Council of Mages. I have killed men who thought themselves gods. I have died but once, to Ashhur himself. There is no shame in your defeat."

Aurelia struggled to her feet. The well of magic inside her was dry. In time, her strength would return, but she doubted the necromancer would give her a day to rest. She used a bit of the magic she did have left to summon her staff. If she were to die, she would die fighting any way she knew how.

The man in black paused, extended his hands, and began to cast. He would give her no chance to strike.

A blade stabbed his side. Velixar whirled, his speed far beyond any mortal. He stepped past Felewen's slash and slammed a hand against her chest. Dark magic poured in. Her arms and legs arched backward, her sword fell from her hand, and her mouth opened in a single, aching shriek. Bits of darkness flared from her mouth, her eyes, and her nostrils.

Done, Velixar shoved her smoking body back into the alley and left her to die. When he turned, he snarled. Aurelia was gone.

"You have delayed me my kill," he said to Felewen's body. "Pray you are dead before I return."

He placed his hood back over his head, pulled it down to cover his features, and then began his search for the sorceress.

15

One after another the deft strokes came in, and one after another Antonil batted them away using the methodical style that had helped him rise to his place at the top of the Neldaren army. His opponent, a young elf whose swordplay was raw compared to most of his brethren, tried to give him no reprieve. The guard captain didn't falter in the slightest.

"You sacrifice planning and thought for sheer speed and reflexes," he said, his breathing steady and practiced. He assumed the elf spoke the human tongue, and the sudden killing lunge proved him correct.

Antonil pulled his head back, the point stopping just shy of drawing blood. An upward cut took the blade from the elf's hand. Antonil's sword looped around, thrust forward, and buried deep inside flesh. The elf fell, gasping for air from the fatal wound. Blood pooled below him. Antonil pulled his sword free and saluted him with the blade.

"Well fought," he said. An arrow clanged against his sword and ricocheted off.

"A warning for your honor," said a camouflaged elf as he stepped out from behind a door. A second arrow followed the first, thudding against Antonil's shield. "A second out of respect." He drew a third. The guard captain charged, his shield leading. While his upper body was covered, nothing stopped the arrow from flying underneath and piercing through the metal greaves protecting his shins. Antonil stumbled, pain flaring up his right leg. He forced himself to continue running. If he could close the gap, the bow would prove no match for his longsword.

Another arrow struck an inch from his left foot. His leg was aflame, yet he continued to charge, pulling back his shield so his sword could lash out. But the elf was not close enough, and he was more skilled with a bow than in just firing arrows. He snapped the wood up, cracking Antonil across the bottom of his hand, which held firm to his blade.

Undaunted, the elf stepped closer, ducked underneath the guard captain's return swing, and then kicked at the arrow still lodged in his shin, finally making Antonil drop his blade.

The elf stood, drawing an arrow as he did. Antonil, now lying on the ground, struggled to bring his shield over his chest. Part of it caught beneath his side and would not come. He would not be able to block in time.

A loud wooden crash stole away the elf's focus. The door to the home behind him exploded into splinters as a huge projectile shot through it. The elf spun, his eyes widening as he saw what had shattered the door: a massacred elven body. He readied his bow and released an arrow at the next sign of movement.

Unfortunately, it was another elven body, curiously missing its left arm and leg. An enormous half-orc in black armor followed, soaked in blood and roaring in mindless fury. He spotted Antonil's attacker, screamed an incomprehensible challenge, and then charged. The elf fired another arrow but was horrified to see it sail high. Behind him, Antonil delivered another kick, this time aiming for the elf's knee instead of his bow.

The elf had to dodge the kick, and that dodge was all it took. The half-orc swung his glowing black blades, cutting his bow, and his body, in twain. As the blood poured free, he roared, looked about, and then ran off toward the sound of combat. A frail form in rags followed from inside the house, a mirror image in looks but for the paler skin and lack of muscle.

"You saw nothing," this second half-orc said to him before following the warrior.

Antonil struggled to his feet, shaking his head all the while.

"It keeps getting stranger," he muttered. He took a step and immediately regretted it. As his leg throbbed, he yanked the arrow out. His armor had kept it from penetrating too deeply, the barbs unable to latch onto any soft flesh. Of course it still hurt like the abyss, but he could deal with that. What he could not deal with, however, was how few in number his soldiers had become. More than four of his own men lay dead around him, joined by three dead elves, five if he counted the two the half-orc had thrown through the doorway. A good ratio considering the skill of the elves, but not good enough. Men he had trained were dying, and for what?

"I have honored your will, my lord," he said. "But it is time I honor my men."

From his belt, he took a white horn bearing the symbol of Neldar. He put this ancient horn to his lips and blew. All throughout Woodhaven rumbled the signal to retreat. He gave the signal two more times before clipping the horn back to his belt and hobbling north.

Aurelia raced down the twisting back alleys of Celed. The dreaded chill of Velixar was far behind her, but still she hesitated to slow. Never before had she felt so vulnerable. As she stopped to catch her breath, a loud horn call echoed throughout the town. The elf sighed, clutching her staff to her chest as she slumped against the side of a house. The battle was over…but would the man in black obey the call?

She thought not.

Suddenly a hand closed about her mouth. The foul smell of sweat and dirt filled her nostrils. An arm reached around, pinning her staff and hands against her chest.

"We may have to leave," a voice growled into her ear, "but I'm not leaving without something to remember."

Aurelia felt her stomach churn. Her assailant turned her around and flung her back against the wall. She glared at a pock-marked soldier bearing the crest of Neldar.

"You're a pretty one," he said, his smile missing several teeth. He yanked at his belt while his other arm pressed against her chest and neck.

"And you're an idiot," she spat. Much of her magic was gone, but not all. Her hand brushed his, and a small shock of electricity crossed between them. The soldier instinctively pulled his hand back, giving Aurelia the opening she needed. She squirmed out from beneath, gripped her staff, and then whirled. The wood cracked against the back of his skull, knocking him against the wall just as hard. Blood splattered from his broken nose.

"You'll pay for--"

The end of her staff dislodged two more of his teeth. The soldier panickedand turned to run, but found his feet entangled. Aurelia marched over, remembering how difficult it had been to strike Harruq and how strong a blow he could take without showing pain.

"Are you as strong as a half-orc?" she asked. Her staff collided with his ribs. He curled up at the blow, crying out in pain. Guess not, she thought. A shove put him on his back. He pleaded to her, sputtering blood, but she ignored him.

"Some people should not reproduce," she said. Down came her staff, all her might behind it. The end smashed his genitals, eliciting a cry of pain beyond anything her spells could do. She continued to strike, punctuating every word with another blow.

"So, let, me, fix, that, for, you!"

She stopped when he passed out from the pain. She turned his head to the side so he wouldn't choke on his own blood, a strange gesture of kindness considering what was left of his manhood.

"Glad to give you something to remember the town by," she said. After a flirtatious flip of her hair, she started down the street.

Aurelia froze, her blood as cold as when she had sensed the man in black. This time no magic could be blamed, and no sense of death. No, it was just the sight of Harruq, dressed in black armor and wielding ancient blades dripping with blood. Just the sight of him massacring an elven warrior.

"Oh, Harruq," she whispered. Then he saw her, and all time stopped.

The two half-orcs heard the sounding of the horn but did not know its purpose. So far from any human soldiers, they could only guess.

"Maybe they're rallying at the horn," Harruq ventured. Qurrah shrugged, glancing down the vacant street in search of victims.

"Perhaps, or perhaps the elves are retreating, or even the humans. Either way, our time is running short. We must find our master. So far no resident of Woodhaven has seen us and lived, but I do not wish to press such luck."

"Looks like we have no choice," Harruq said, crossing his swords in an 'X' before his chest. Far down the street, where the road hooked left like the back leg of a dog, an elven archer approached, his bow ready. Two arrows flew into the air. Both half-orcs dodged as the arrows whistled past.

"Close the distance," Qurrah said before beginning a spell. Harruq charged, bellowing a mindless war cry. The archer fired two more arrows and then bolted around the corner.

"He's seen us!" Harruq shouted, easily veering about the arrows as he increased speed.

"Wait, brother, it might be a trap!"

Qurrah doubled over hacking, his reward for trying to shout so loud. Harruq halted, his head jerking back and forth as he debated what to do. Qurrah glanced up, tried to speak, and then swore as the elf leaned around the corner and fired another arrow. He did his best to dodge, but he was far less mobile than his brother. The arrow pierced between his left shoulder and collarbone, burying the barbed tip deep in his flesh. The half-orc let out a stunned gasp. He staggered right, clutching his shoulder as he slumped against the front of a home.

"Qurrah!" Harruq shrieked, racing to his brother. Qurrah shoved away his clumsy attempts to examine the wound.

"Kill him for me," the necromancer gasped. "Go! He cannot live!"

"But you're bleeding real bad and…"

"I have the healing potions, now go!"

Harruq's gut screamed against the idea, but in the end, he listened to his brother. He drew his swords and gave chase.

Qurrah waited until Harruq was around the corner before taking out one of his small glass vials. Before he could pull the cork off the top, he heard a voice speak.

"So many dead by your hands yet a single arrow nearly takes your life?"

The half-orc froze, the vial clutched in his hands. An elf emerged from behind the building, his body decorated in a brilliant green cloak and silvery armor. It was the same elf who had fired the first warning shot to Antonil before the entire battle had begun.

"I am but a poor outcast," Qurrah said, hiding the handle of the whip underneath the palm of his hand. The coiled leather vibrated, hungering for blood.

"Do not lie to me. I have watched you two slaughter my brethren. I have seen much of your handiwork." The elf glared at him, ugly hatred skewing his handsome features. "By now your brother is dead. Three of my best warriors await him around that corner. I thought it appropriate you knew this before I took your life."

"Do not talk to me of what is appropriate," Qurrah said. "Kill me, if you will, but do not bore me with your chatter. I have suffered beyond anything you can do to me."

A firestorm of anger overwhelmed the elf's features. He stepped back and drew an arrow. Qurrah lashed his whip, but his speed was not enough. An arrow tore right through his hand. The whip fell, the fire vanishing the second it left contact with Qurrah's skin.

A second arrow followed. The half-orc rocked backward, his brown eyes wide in shock, as the tip pierced deep into his throat. The healing potion fell from his hands and broke against a rock. He slid back, resting against a home as he gasped for breath.

The elf grabbed the shaft of the arrow, and that sick anger filled his face.

"How many of my kin died to your hand?" he asked. A twist of his hand sent spasms of pain all throughout Qurrah's body. He coughed violently, and blood ran down his lips and neck.

"Don't feel like answering?" the elf mocked. "Why did you kill them? For money? Power? How many died to better your miserable excuse of a life?"

Another twist. Qurrah leaned forward, clutching at his tormenter's shaking hands. Words spilled from the half-orc's mouth, garbled and nearly unintelligible.

"What is it you wish to say to me?" the elf asked, ignoring the flailing hands that pawed at his face.

"*Hemorrhage*," the half-orc hissed.

The elf's face exploded.

Qurrah fell over onto his side, breathing as slowly as he could through the blood that filled his throat. The dead body of the elf crumpled in front of him, all of his hate-filled features gone from his face except for a single eye. The half-orc stared, wondering if his brother was truly dead.

Darkness crept at the corner of his sight. His strength was fading fast, and he had little doubt that if he passed out he would never wake. He struggled to lift a single numb hand, then flopped it down on top of the dead elf's leg.

Qurrah took as deep a breath as he dared and then spoke the words of a spell. Each syllable was slow torture, garbled in blood and born of pain most horrid. Thankfully, the spell was not complicated, and the words were few. He finished the spell mere seconds before his mind succumbed to the sleep that crawled at his eyes.

Even though he was dead, life energy still swirled inside the elf's body. Normally this energy would be consumed by the earth in burial, but Qurrah had other plans. His spell took in this life energy through his hand, filling his body with it, healing his wounds and clearing his mind. The darkness fighting for control in his head subsided, a shred of strength returning to his limbs.

There was still the slight problem of the arrow lodged in his throat. Qurrah had a solution but it was far from pleasant. Most likely he would die, but he had to try. He heard no screams coming from around the corner, but he knew that meant nothing. He had to believe his brother was still alive. He had to help him.

Qurrah took out his last healing potion, popped the cork, and then held it before him. Blood was beginning to fill his throat once more. His stolen energy was quickly fading. He had no time to waste. He tilted his head as high as the arrow in his neck allowed, positioned the mouth of the vial against his lower lip, and then closed his hand around the arrow shaft. One last hissing breath. One tremble of his fingers. He yanked the arrow out.

Sheer reflex kept him alive. His head shot backward and his arm went limp. The potion tilted enough so that half spilled down his throat. With the pain so unbearable, he dared not cough against the liquid that came burning down. Some of it went into his lungs, but he kept them still.

Qurrah reclined, closed his eyes, and let the potion do its work. He could feel the magic flowing through his body, concentrating about his ruined throat. Part of him hoped the liquid would heal the damage done so many years ago, but he knew better. A scar that old was beyond repair. He would have to settle for surviving. That was just fine with him.

When he finally dared a loud, gasping breath of air, the pain was not so bad. Qurrah stood, picked up his whip, and then went to help his brother. He expected to see his body dead in the street, for why else had he still not returned? He held hope that Harruq still fought against his enemies, or that more had come beyond the three the elf had claimed.

What he was not prepared for was the sight of Harruq hunched over the dying body of Aurelia Thyne.

"Harruq," he tried to call out. The flesh in the back of his throat tore. Blood poured down his throat, slick and hot. Qurrah cursed. Such a wound would kill him if he did not seek help. He needed to steal more life, and for that, he needed another body. He glanced behind. The dead elf was dry, but far down the street were two more he and his brother had killed.

He glanced once more to Harruq. Three elves lay dead about him. He could use them, knew he should use them, but something turned him away. It was the look on his brother's face. He could not bear to see it.

Qurrah hobbled to where two bodies full of life energy awaited his coming.

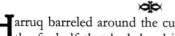

Harruq barreled around the curve, determined to catch the foul elf that had dared injure his brother. As he turned the corner, the twang of bowstrings filled the air. Three arrows hit his chest, barely puncturing his armor. He bellowed, furious. All three elves were in the center of the street, away from cover or protection. They would die, all of them.

The archers fired another volley as if not surprised the first three had done little but anger him. One zipped by his head as he ran, two others thudding into his chest and arm. Blood soaked the inside of his armor, but the wounds were superficial, halted by the magical leather before penetrating deep enough to be a bother.

"For the head," the closest elf shouted in his native tongue. He managed one last shot before Harruq closed the distance. The half-orc batted the arrow away without thinking.

"You bastard!" he shouted, slamming into the elf without pausing. He buried his swords deep into the elf's chest as he plowed forward. "You hurt my brother! You spineless cowards!" The other two abandoned their bows and drew their blades.

"Your brother is dead," one elf said. "Gaelwren waited for your departure. He will not find it difficult killing a wounded dog."

The anger inside Harruq consumed him entirely. He charged the elf, abandoning any hint of precaution. He slammed his blades down with all his might. The elf blocked once, twice, then three times, wincing each time he did. Then the other elf was behind Harruq, stabbing at his back. While mad with rage, Harruq still knew very well where his opponents were.

He spun, avoiding the thrust, and then trapped his assailant's arm with his elbow. A flex of his muscles cracked bone, and the sword fell from a limp hand. Harruq let him go, bellowed at the first elf, and then hurled both his blades. They turned end over end through the air, one missing, one not. The one that missed sailed until it hit ground and bounced. The hilt of the one that did not smacked him hard in the forehead.

The elf staggered back, swiping at Harruq as the half-orc charged. A thin line of blood appeared on the half-orc's forehead, but he was oblivious to it. His hands were around his enemy's throat and his strength at its greatest. The crunching flesh underneath his fingers was all that mattered. The elf behind him retrieved his sword and attacked, his right arm hanging useless, his left stabbing desperately. Harruq flung the dying body around by the neck. The sword buried up to the hilt in the makeshift shield.

Harruq dropped the dead elf and lashed out. His backhand broke the elf's jaw. Reeling, the elf staggered back, only able to raise his meager arm above his head. Harruq smashed an elbow into his chest, followed by knuckled fists atop his skull.

"Stay down," Harruq said. He retrieved Salvation and Condemnation from the dirt, and then stomped over to the beaten, bloody elf warrior.

"Mercy, I am beaten," the elf gasped as Harruq lifted his head by the hair.

"No such thing," he said. Salvation tore out his throat. Condemnation hacked off his head. He sheathed his blades, breathed in deeply, and then let it all out in an ecstatic, primal cry. As the last of it left his lips, he saw an elf's shocked walnut eyes from a nearby alley. His gut lurched. The fire in his veins sputtered.

"Why so surprised?" he asked Aurelia, shame draining the thrill of his kill.

"How could you?" she asked him. "What harm have we done to you?"

Harruq shrugged. "You think you know me, but you don't. I kill, Aurry. It's what I do. It's what I do best." He drew out his swords, still dripping with blood. "Perhaps you didn't believe it, but this is me."

"Don't do this," Aurelia said softly. "It doesn't have to be this way. Please, Harruq. I don't want to fight you."

"I didn't want you to fight either," Harruq said, his eyes leaving hers for an instant. He took a step toward her and raised his swords, just as when they sparred.

"Stop this," Aurelia said. Her staff remained at her side. "Will you kill me, too?"

"I asked you not to fight, but here you are. Qurrah made it simple, Aurry. Either I love you or I kill you."

Sparks rained down as he clanged his swords together.

"Is that how you feel?" she asked. The tears in her eyes ran down her cheeks, not to be replaced by any more.

"So be it." She took up her staff and held it defensively. "You are a fool, Harruq. May you die as one."

Harruq charged, his black blades gleaming. Every nagging doubt, every tiny part screaming for him to sheath his blades, he channeled into his mindless rage. His swords hacked chunks out of the staff, which held together only by Aurelia's powerful enchantments. She blocked several attack routines but one finally slipped past. her dodge too slow, a black blade cut across her cheek. She paused, rubbing her cheek as Harruq smirked.

Blood. It was as she feared. Harruq's weapons were enchanted.

"Your spells won't save you," he shouted. "No elf will save you. No one!"

"Why this hatred?" she asked, smacking away a dual thrust. "When have I shown you anything but kindness?"

Harruq gave her no answer. Instead, he stabbed with Salvation, a higher thrust of Condemnation trailing behind it. Aurelia turned her staff horizontal and pushed upward. Both swords stabbed high above her head. A quick turn and one end of her staff rammed the half-orc in the gut. The blow knocked the wind out of Harruq.

"For what reason do we fight?" she asked. "For what reason do you harbor this hatred?"

He glared. "I told you. I'm fighting elves. You're one of them. No simpler than that."

"Liar."

Harruq snarled, the elf inside him all but invisible. He charged, recklessly hacking at Aurelia.

"Why do we fight?" she asked again, desperately trying to block every swing. Blood covered her arms, and another swing cut through her dress, slicing into the beautiful flesh of her leg. "Why, Harruq? Why!"

"I don't know!" he cried. Strength surged into him, dark and unholy. In the blink of an eye, he twirled both swords, knocked Aurelia's staff from her hand, and then looped his right arm all the way around to bury Condemnation deep into her stomach.

Everything, all fighting, all arguing, all bleeding, living and dying halted at that moment. For Harruq, there was only the sight of Aurelia doubled over, her eyes filled with sadness. His arm yanked the blade out of her, without any thought on his part.

"Harruq?" she gasped. She fell on her back, still clutching her bleeding abdomen.

That look of sadness tore through his rage. What should have been the exhilaration of the kill was instead the cold, biting emotion of guilt. His eyes lingered on the blood on his blade before something changed inside. He looked back to the elf, and again the words of his brother echoed in his head.

Do you love her?

No, he'd said.

Then kill her.

"Aurelia?" he asked, as if seeing her for the first time. "I didn't mean to, I, Aurry, please…"

He knelt down, his blades falling from his limp hands. He pulled away Aurelia's hand to see the blood, to see the wound.

"No," he said. He rocked backward, the color draining from his face. "No, I didn't mean to, I didn't…I didn't…"

Aurelia tried to say something, tried to comfort him, but no noise came from her throat. She was dying.

"No!" Harruq shouted. He pulled out one of his healing potions, yanked off the cork, and forced the contents down Aurelia's throat. The elf gagged, retching up half of it onto her neck and chest. Harruq got out his last potion but could not open it for the shaking of his hands. Desperate, he put it down, picked up one of his swords, and shattered the top of the vial. He flung the potion back to Aurelia's mouth, nearly shredding her lower lip on the broken glass. More of the silvery-blue liquid poured down her throat.

Harruq sat there, clutching her hands in his and waiting. The seconds crawled slower than the longest of years. He didn't care if anyone came and saw him, not even his brother. His tears fell onto her bloodstained dress. For far too long, she did not move. His heart cried out in agony. It was too late. He had killed her.

"I'm so sorry," he whispered to her. "Forgive me, please, if you can…"

"What are you babbling about?" the elf asked, her eyes cracking open. Harruq tried to smile, but a sob came out instead. He hugged her, his forehead pressed against hers.

"Help me up," she said. Harruq did as commanded. When she was standing, he grabbed his blades and sheathed them. She leaned all her weight against him, and such close contact only deepened his guilt and anger. He knew she watched him, and he wiped away his tears as quickly and subtly as he could.

"Why, Harruq?" she asked him. The half-orc shrugged.

"We…Qurrah…I don't know."

"No," she said, leaning on her staff. "Why did you save me?"

He kicked his toes into the dirt, unable to piece together the chaotic mess inside his head and heart. All he could think of was what his brother had told him to do.

"Qurrah said to kill you if I didn't love you…"

"Yet you didn't," she said. Harruq nodded, but said nothing else.

"*Hana fael!*" a voice cried from far down the alley. Both turned to see an elf raise his bow and fire.

"Look out," Aurelia said, shoving Harruq aside. The arrow hit her breast and reflected off as if hitting stone. She glanced at Harruq, her face a mixture of anger and fear.

"Others have seen you kill, haven't they?" she asked.

Harruq could only shrug. More shouts came as two other elves turned the corner. Aurelia swore as she heard what they said.

"They call me traitor," she said. "I protected you, and now I am a traitor."

The half-orc stepped before her, preparing his swords. "They won't touch you."

"I know," Aurelia said, summoning the last bit of magic inside her. A tear in the fabric of reality ripped open, swirling with white and blue magic.

"Get in," she yelled.

"What about Qurrah?" he shouted.

"Go inside, you dumb fool!"

She cracked her staff across his back. Harruq stumbled into the portal and vanished. Aurelia stepped in after, arrows landing all around her.

Qurrah watched the blue portal close, leaving him alone and hunted in a town full of enemies.

"Brother, how could you?" he asked, dread clutching his throat. Elves were running down the alley, yelling in their language. Qurrah ducked back around, cursed his brother, and then darted to the nearest home. The first one had locks, as did the second, but the third was unbarred. He hid inside as the shouts of search parties went rushing past.

Qurrah climbed the stairs to the second floor, sat down beside a bed, and then in silence pondered his fate now that he was alone.

16

Far from town, a blue portal tore open above empty grass. The big half-orc tumbled out, followed by a flustered Aurelia. Upon her exit, the portal closed, swirling away as if it had never existed. Harruq groaned, spitting out dirt that had made its way into his mouth.

"Where are we?" he asked.

"About two miles east of Woodhaven," she told him. Harruq glanced around, unable to see the town in the distance.

"So that's how you always showed up behind me," he said as he got to his feet. "That magic...blue thingie?"

"That magic blue thingie is a portal," Aurelia said, her arms crossed over her chest as she held her elbows. "And yes, that is how I did it."

Harruq shrugged, glancing about as he tried to get his bearings. A thought hit him, harder than any whacks of Aurelia's staff.

"Qurrah!" he gasped. "You've got to send me back."

"I can't," Aurelia said, her eyes fixed west.

"What do you mean you can't?" He stormed over and grabbed her arms. "Send me back, I'm telling you to! Qurrah's all alone, and they'll kill him if I don't help him!"

"I can't, Harruq, I can't!" she shouted, pulling back from his hands. "I have no strength left to open another portal. You, and he, will have to wait until I get some rest."

"How long will that be?"

"Tomorrow morning," she said.

He raged and sputtered but could think of nothing to say or do. Finally, he started walking.

"Where are you going?" she asked him.

"To get my brother," he said without turning around.

"They will kill you," she shouted. "They will see you and kill you. You do your brother nothing by running off to die."

"Then what am I supposed to do?" he screamed. He whirled around, his helplessness showing on every feature of his face.

"Have faith in him," she said. She pulled a strand of hair from her face as the wind blew against her. "I have given up everything for you, Harruq. Don't you see that? My friends, my family, my home; they are all gone from me. Because of you. Don't make it all for nothing."

Harruq's anger and frustration simmered and swirled in a dying fire. He could not argue with her, not about that. Even he could see what she had sacrificed to save his life.

"Where do we go?" he asked, his voice revealing his defeat.

"We'll figure it out in the morning. For now, we travel north. Your brother will be fine, I promise."

He nodded but said nothing. The two traveled in between the hills, exhausted but unwilling to stop their movement.

"Why did you fight the elves?" she asked when their silence had stretched for more than half an hour.

"It'll be a long story," he said.

"We have time."

He chuckled. "Aye, I guess we do."

He told her of Velixar and his plans. He told her of the strength, weapons, and armor granted to him. Hesitantly, he recounted killing Ahrqur and the people of Cornrows, a fresh wave of shame filling him as he thought of both.

"What part did Ahrqur play in this?" Aurelia asked. "Was he enlisted by Velixar?"

Harruq shook his head. "Me and Qurrah killed him, then Velixar brought him back and sent him off to the king. It was very much unwilling on his part. That guy was me and Qurrah's dad, you know that? We killed our own dad, and never even knew it while we did."

She frowned, and deep lines of exhaustion marred her beauty.

"Tonight we need to have a serious talk," she said. "For now, I'd prefer we speak of lighter things."

"Sure thing," he said. They spoke no word of Woodhaven, Velixar, or the battle that morning for the rest of the day.

The sound of an opening door stirred him from his slumber. Qurrah glanced around, furious that he had fallen asleep. How much time had passed? An hour? Five?

"I cannot be so weak," he muttered to himself. Footsteps echoed from the first floor. One person, he guessed, most likely an elf judging by the design of the building. Qurrah stood and readied his whip. He would not cower in hiding. This was his home now. He would defend it.

"You are not safe here," Qurrah whispered. "For if you are safe, then I am not."

He crept down the stairs, the whip coiled and ready to burst into flame. Before the circular front window stood an elf, one hand on the glass, the other holding a bow. Qurrah reached into his pocket, clutching a few pieces of bone. Before he could draw them out the elf spoke, his voice soft and sad.

"Too much death this day," he said. "For hundreds of years my brother and I lived here, and for hundreds of years more we would have remained. He is dead now, and for what reason?"

"Death has no reason," Qurrah said, his whole body tensing.

"No," the elf said, turning around so he could stare at Qurrah eye to eye. "But murderers do."

Neither moved. Neither spoke. Qurrah felt his nerves fray, and in his gut a sudden confusion swelled. He felt as if he hung over the side of a cliff, and the bones he held were the rope. The elf let go of his bow and held his hands out to either side.

"No more have to die," the elf said. The flesh around his eyes sagged wearily, and he leaned against the window to aid in standing. It was as if grief had rendered him lifeless.

Let go, Qurrah thought. He could let go. Fall down the cliff, and find what awaited him at the bottom. All he had to do was let go of the bones. The confusion burned hotter in his gut.

"You're right," Qurrah said, standing to his full height. "No more have to die. But what we do doesn't matter, for more always will."

He opened his hands. Fueled by dark magic, the bones shot forth, piercing the elf's throat and eyes. Against the window his dying body fell, his arms still held wide as if offering an embrace that would never be returned. Qurrah stared at the corpse, and as the blood pooled on the floor he felt himself standing once more on solid ground. The elves were his enemy. His brother was his only friend. Velixar was his master. Solid ground.

Qurrah slipped over to the window and glanced out. The sun hung low, its top edge barely visible above the rooftops. He had hoped the streets would be empty, but instead he saw a patrol of elves turn the corner, their swords drawn. He stepped back and hid as they passed by. The half-orc chewed on his fingers. Harruq had abandoned him, true, but perhaps he remained nearby, waiting for him. Then there was Velixar, no doubt furious at the elves' victory. Where did Karak's prophet linger now that the battle had ended?

There was only one way to find out. He would have to escape the town, regardless of the patrols that swarmed the area.

He waited until nightfall. Even in the dark the elves still patrolled, carrying no torches for their keen eyes had no trouble seeing in the starlight. The longer he hid and watched, the more Qurrah was convinced they searched for him. The Neldaren troops were long gone, Harruq with them. He knew he was being paranoid, but the only other person they could be searching for was Velixar, and the elves were deluding themselves if they thought they could handle him.

When a smaller patrol turned a corner and vanished, he opened the door, winked at the bloody corpse near the window, and then slipped into the night. The scent of mourning floated throughout the town, and he paused to enjoy the bittersweet strands of death that tugged on his heart. So many souls lost in battle, and even in the quiet aftermath, it was intoxicating.

"No sleep tonight," he said, turning back to the building that had been his shelter. Fire swarmed around his fingers. Like streams of water, it flowed from his hands, splashing across the roof and setting it ablaze. Finished, he ran for an alley to hide as the fire gained the attention of the many patrols. He heard footsteps and shouts further down the road so he ducked left, running in between homes as all around the shouts grew louder.

The houses ended, and like a fleeing thief he burst out into the streets only to slam into a drunken man holding a small bottle. The two rolled, a tangle of legs and arms. The small bottle shattered.

"What the abyss are you..." the man started to say, but Qurrah's hand pressed against his lips.

"Your voice or your life," Qurrah said, danger flaring in his eyes. The half-orc pushed him away and got to his feet. He glanced around, trying to orientate himself, when he felt a sharp pain stab into his back. He spun, his whip lashing out as it burst into flame. It wrapped around the man's neck, choking out death cries as his flesh seared and smoke filled his lungs. The only noise Qurrah heard was the sound of skin blistering and popping in the fire. At last the man crumpled, the bloodied shard of glass from the bottle still in his hand.

"Damn it," Qurrah said, wincing as he touched the cut on his back. It was wide but not deep. Painful too, he noticed as he took a few steps. Furious, he turned back to the corpse of the drunken man and smashed a fist against its chest. The body shriveled into dust, only the bones remaining.

"Halt!" shouted a voice from far down the street. Qurrah glimpsed an elf carrying a bow. Just one, the half-orc noticed, but that would quickly change.

"Perhaps you'll have some use after all," Qurrah said to the bones. He whispered words of magic as the elf took a few steps closer and notched an arrow. A purple fire surrounded the bones, pulled them into the air, and then hurled them in a giant wave. The elf released his own arrow, but Qurrah was faster. He dove to the side as the arrow clacked against the stone. The elf tried batting the bones away, but he was a fool, unaware of the strength guiding them. They shattered his bow, crashed into his slender form, and tore flesh and armor.

"Kill him," Qurrah said to the bones. They swirled in the air above the elf like a tornado, and all at once they plunged downward, deep into his flesh.

More shouts. He turned north and ran deeper into Singhelm. He doubted any humans patrolled the area, not after the defeat of their army. If he was to find safety, it would be there. In each ragged breath, he gasped, tasting copper on his tongue. His back ached, and his whole body revolted against his constant motion. Still, he had no choice. He passed by home after home, each one dark and quiet. It seemed the occupants of Singhelm were terrified the elves might seek vengeance for the king's edict. Qurrah chuckled though it felt like hammers pummeled his chest.

He spread his hands to either side and bathed a few houses with fire. The city's fear was deep enough he could sense it like a cold breeze, and he wanted it to deepen.

An arrow whistled by, clipping his ear. Qurrah dropped to his knees as a second thudded into the side of a home, inches from his neck. A spell on his lips, he spun, grabbing chunks of dirt in his hands to use as components for a spell. From two windows, a pair of elves held bows, and together they pulled back the strings and released their arrows. The ground beneath Qurrah cracked and tore as his spell completed, so that he fell into a deep pit. The landing jarred his back, and he gasped for air, but for the moment he was safe from the arrows that went flying above.

The fire continued to spread. Qurrah could see its flickers of light, and even in his little pit he felt the heat. His whole body ached, and he wished nothing more than to lay there like a corpse in a grave, but he had no time. He needed to take care of the meddlesome elves that had him pinned.

"Like shadows in the night," he whispered, remembering how Velixar had described a certain spell to him. "Shadows that vanish and reappear at will."

He spoke the words and poured his power into them. He felt his body shift, and his sight twisted so that he saw many things. A spider, he thought. Velixar should have told him it was like becoming a spider. A mere thought of moving sent him spiraling, reappearing place to place. Ending the spell left him totally disoriented. His sight returned to normal, and it felt a little like falling from a very tall tree. As he retched on his knees, he looked about, discerning his location. He was beside the building the two elves were in, directly underneath their windows. He could see the tips of their arrows sticking out, glinting in torchlight.

Two adjacent homes were already ablaze, their occupants still inside. Qurrah turned and grabbed the frame of the door.

"Burn!" he shouted, loud enough for the elves to hear. The wood blackened, smoke billowed from his hands, and then the entire building erupted as if bathed in oil. Qurrah laughed, untouched by the heat. He could not say the same for the elves, and as their pained screams reached his ears he only laughed louder.

The half-orc ran as people flooded the streets, calling out for buckets and water. Too many homes were aflame.

They could no longer cower within them and hope to be spared. In the commotion, Qurrah vanished, unseen and uncared for. He had spent his whole life disappearing in crowds, and in the dark of night, surrounded by fear and worry, he was just a shadow.

✣

Qurrah was in no hurry as he left the city behind. The grass was soft and tall, and it felt good under his feet after so much sprinting down stone roads. Stars filled the sky, and he smiled to them often. In the distance, he spotted a small fire, and he knew to whom it belonged.

"Where is your brother?" Velixar asked as Qurrah approached.

"He has abandoned me," Qurrah said, pulling at his robes. He glanced back to the town, hoping to change the topic. Velixar's gaze followed his, and together they noticed the smell floating in the breeze.

"There are bodies nearby," Qurrah said. "Hundreds. I can feel them."

"Elves do not bury their kin," Velixar whispered. "The few tombs they do build house nothing but ash. Instead, they pile the bodies of the dead to burn, but not tonight. Tonight they mourn." He stood erect, stretching out his arms as if relishing the warmth of sunshine. "Such wonderful dead. To die in combat is a glorious fate, Qurrah. Never forget it. The blessings of gods linger in those who fight and fall valiantly."

Qurrah nodded. He could feel power creeping out of his master, cold and fierce. Soft purple dust flew from his pale hands.

"The trust between man and elf is broken," Velixar said. "Let the harvest of their distrust begin."

Arcane words of power flowed from Velixar. Qurrah knew them, knew their purpose. They were the exact same words he had used to raise the eight undead at Cornrows. The only difference, however, was in the power Velixar gave them. Each word rolled forth like some unstoppable wave, deep and resonating. He relished the feel, knowing that one day he would speak the words in such a manner.

Velixar lifted his hands to the sky, shouting out the last of the spell. The final command came shrieking forth from his lips.

"*Rise!*"

In the distance, dark shapes rose from the grass. Four hundred bodies of men and elves marched silently away from town, back toward their master. Qurrah smiled. The macabre sight was beautiful.

"What shall you do with them?" he asked.

"They will join my army. Two thousand I now have. We are close. So close. Soon we will have enough to crush Veldaren."

"Where is this army?"

Velixar flashed an ugly smile. "They are with me always."

As if this very comment brought forth their existence, thousands of decaying, mindless beings surrounded them.

"How can you command so many?" Qurrah gasped.

"You will learn. Come. We must put as much distance as we can between us and Woodhaven."

The hundreds from Woodhaven joined the thousands. Flanked in an army of undead, the necromancers trekked north.

"Clever," Dieredon whispered from atop Sonowin, watching the undead army's departure. They circled back, returning to the Erze forest nestled around Woodhaven. Dieredon had returned too late to find and assault Velixar, so instead he had kept his troops hidden and waiting. The battle ended as he had hoped, and even Antonil had survived, Celestia be praised. The elf glanced back, memorizing the exact direction the undead marched. "Clever, and disgusting," he added. "Death is nothing but a recruitment tool for you."

Half an hour later, he and a hundred other elves riding atop pegasi followed the necromancer north. As they flew, they passed over a small campfire dotting the empty field below. Their passage above went unheard and unseen, for the two lone souls sitting on opposite sides of that campfire were deep in conversation.

><|><

"Harruq, I want you to make me a promise."
"And what is that?"

Aurelia leaned back and tucked a few strands of hair behind her ear as high above the stars sparkled sadly.

"Promise you will never strike at me, or those close to me, ever again."

The half-orc shifted uncomfortably in the grass. "You know I'd never do that."

"No, Harruq, I don't know. I think I know, I desperately want to believe I know, but I don't. So promise me."

"Aurry…"

"Promise me now, or I will drag you back to the elves and let them deal the justice you deserve."

Harruq glared into the fire. It was such an easy promise, but could he keep it? What if Velixar ordered otherwise, or someone close to Aurelia struck against Qurrah?

He sighed. In his heart, he knew he could never again strike at Aurelia, regardless of what anyone else wanted of him. The look on her face when he had stabbed her, that combination of sadness and shock, would haunt him forever.

"Fine," he said. "I promise. Happy?"

"Far from it."

Aurelia crossed her legs, tossed back her hair, and then leaned her head on her hands as she stared into the fire.

"I want you to listen to me, alright Harruq?"

"Sure."

He glanced down, uncomfortable and saddened that Aurelia refused to look him in the eye.

"Velixar is not who you think he is. He isn't *what* you think he is. He tried to kill me, Harruq. He enjoyed every second we fought. I saw many of my friends die at his hand. Do you know why he helps you? Why he claims to train you?"

She gave no pause, no chance for him to answer. This was good, for he didn't want to. Too much was on his mind for argument. He remained quiet and listened.

"He wants to change you, turn you into what you know he is. A murderer without guilt. Without conscience. A living weapon to be used however he wants you to be used."

Harruq's heart sped up a few paces as Aurelia rose and walked over to where he sat. She knelt down and rubbed a soft hand against his face. She finally looked into his eyes.

"You are not a weapon, Harruq. You are a kind, intelligent half-elf. You always have a choice. Never forget that."

She kissed his cheek. His heart skipped. When she sat back down, he looked down at his brutish hands and muscles. She noticed and crossed her arms.

"Velixar's gift," she said. "Do you still desire it?"

Harruq closed his eyes, his fingers shaking. Deep within his chest, he felt a rage steadily growing. When Velixar had first given the strength to him, he'd felt an overwhelming desire to use it. Anger swelled inside, and when he looked to Aurelia he felt an enormous desire to attack. She was questioning his master, his brother, questioning what it meant to be him.

When he opened his eyes, Aurelia stood, shocked by the red light wafting like smoke from Harruq's eyes.

"You could never know what I am," he said.

"I've seen what you can be," she said. "Is that not enough?"

The words stung him. His vision swam crimson. He felt his hands close upon his swords. Perhaps he shouldn't have saved her. Perhaps he should have left her bleeding upon the ground to die alone and…

"No!" he screamed, flinging himself to his knees. He drew his swords and flung them aside, not daring to have their touch near him just then. Velixar's voice throbbed in his ears, a chant of promises and loyalty.

"Deny the gift," Aurelia said, the faintest hint of magic on her fingertips. "Give me some shred of hope."

He closed his eyes. Tears trickled down his face. He felt the anger growing inside him, but he forced it down. In his mind's eye, he saw Velixar. The old prophet warned of death, retribution, and pain, but Harruq silenced him. Let the gift be gone. He denied the darkness within him. If this was betrayal, then so be it. He would pay the cost.

Great spasms racked his body. All the power Velixar had granted him fled. His muscles shrank inward, tightening in great, painful shudders. Several minutes passed as the horrendous pain tore through his arms, chest, and legs. Aurelia held him as he lay sobbing in pain. She did her best to comfort him, stroking his hair until all his dark strength drained away. Exhaustion came soon after, and for an agonizing time Harruq lay there, mumbling incoherently and waiting for the pain to fade.

At last, he looked up to Aurelia, his eyes a calm brown, the whites bloodshot.

"I love you," he said.

Sleep took him, and relieved, Aurelia let her own eyes close and her hair drape across his face.

◈

"Wake up, Qurrah."

The half-orc lifted his eyelids to see the thoroughly unwelcoming sight of Velixar frowning down at him.

"Yes, master?" he asked, puzzled, for it was still before dawn. He had slept no more than a few hours, he figured.

"Who is it your brother travels with now?" Velixar asked. "You say he has abandoned you, but to whom?"

"An elf named Aurelia," Qurrah said as he sat up. He rubbed his eyes, still feeling groggy. "Why do you ask?"

"Because he has rejected us, my disciple," Velixar said. "His strength has left him. My heart burns with this betrayal, and I must know who to punish."

Qurrah felt ill at ease. All around him, the sea of undead swayed and moaned as if they shared their master's anger.

"Perhaps it is a mistake," he said. "Or he has done so only to keep himself safe. Let me talk to him. He will listen to me; he always has."

Velixar shook his head and pointed toward Woodhaven in the far distance.

"Back there he left you, and I must punish him for such...Qurrah, look to the sky."

Qurrah followed Velixar's gaze, and there in the distance he saw many white objects faintly illuminated by the stars.

"About a hundred," Qurrah said. "But what are they?"

"Elves," the man in black said. "And I know who leads them. Prepare yourself, my disciple. I have erred, and now we pay the price."

Qurrah nodded, then closed his eyes and rehearsed the spells he knew. They were weak compared to his master's but they would claim a few lives. His whip curled around his arm, ready for more bloodshed. The white dots in the distance grew at a frightening rate.

"Such speed," Qurrah said. "How?"

"They are the ekreissar," Velixar answered. "The Quellan elite are the only ones capable of raising and flying the winged horses. When they fly in, stay low, and aim your spells for their horses. The rider will die from the fall."

The man in black closed his eyes and spoke to the undead surrounding them.

"Hide our presence," he ordered. "Spread about, and do not halt your movement for all eternity."

The two thousand obeyed, scattering in a constantly moving jumble of arms and legs.

"That should help keep our presence hidden for a time," Qurrah said.

"They are but distractions. The darkness will hide us from their arrows."

Before Qurrah could ask what Velixar meant, his master was already in the midst of another spell. Inky darkness rose all about his feet, swirling like black floodwaters. Chills crept up his ankles as the liquid darkness grew. Velixar cried out the final words of the spell, spreading the darkness for a mile in all directions, so high it covered up to their necks.

"It is cold," Qurrah said, his teeth chattering.

"You will not be harmed by it," Velixar said, watching the approaching army. "With so much hidden, they will be hard pressed to target us among my undead. Hold nothing back. They are here."

"What should we do?" one elf shouted above the wind roaring past their ears.

"Unleash our arrows," Dieredon shouted back. "Watch for the necromancer. Ignore the undead once you locate him."

The blasphemous blanket of darkness stretched out below them like a great fog, filled with bobbing heads of Velixar's army. In that chaotic mass, Dieredon knew the man in black would remain well hidden. Not until enough of the undead had been massacred.

He readied his bow, his strong legs the only thing holding him to Sonowin. Three arrows pressed against the string of the bow, their tips dipped in holy water. His quiver, as was the quiver of every elf flying alongside him, contained water given to them by their clerics of Celestia. When their arrows bit into dead flesh, it would be like fire on a dry leaf.

"Let no life lost this night be in vain!" Dieredon cried as they descended like a white river, raining arrows into the darkness. More than two hundred moving forms halted after that one pass, but a thousand more swayed in their sick, distracting dance.

"One free pass," Velixar said, observing the flight of elves as they swarmed overhead. They banked around, still in perfect formation, and then dove again.

"Kill them now!" he ordered, his fingers crooking into strange shapes.

"*Hemorrhage!*" Qurrah hissed, pointing at the nearest horse. Blood ruptured from the beautiful creature's neck. The rider steadied her best he could, knowing his doom approached. They crashed into the inky blackness, crushing bodies underneath before the swarming dead tore them to pieces.

Velixar's first attack was far more impressive. Bits of bone ripped out from his undead army; femurs, fingers, ribs, and teeth flew into the sky in a deadly assault. The elves broke formation as the barrage approached. The first ten, however, were too close to have hope. Bone shredded wings and scattered feathers. The elves that were alive when their horses landed died by the clawing hands of rotted flesh.

Dieredon looped in the sky, his confidence shaken at the sight of so many of his dying friends. He fired arrows three at a time, his quiver never approaching empty. He ordered Sonowin lower, shouting out the command as another barrage of bone pelted four more elves to their deaths. Skimming above the darkness, Dieredon fired volley after volley behind him. When they were past the undead, he pulled Sonowin high into the air to observe the battlefield.

The ranks of the undead were half of what they had been, yet still he could not see the lowered black hood he so badly needed to see.

"Come, Sonowin, we will find him, even if it means killing every last one of his puppets."

The horse neighed and dove, spurred on by the sight of its own kind falling in death.

⊰✧⊱

"Behind you, master," Qurrah said. He hurried the words of a spell as Velixar turned. An incorporeal hand shot from Qurrah's own, flying across the battlefield to where an elf dove toward them, arrows flashing two at a time in the starlight. The hand struck the elf in the chest, freezing flesh and eviscerating his insides with ice. The flying horse banked upward as its master fell limp into the fog.

"Beautiful, Qurrah," Velixar said, bloodlust burning in his red eyes. His precious undead were being massacred. He could feel their numbers dwindling in his mind, now but a third of what his glorious army had been.

"This has gone on long enough," he seethed. He outstretched his hands and shrieked words of magic. Qurrah staggered back, in awe of the power that came rolling forth. The fog of darkness swirled and recoiled at each word Velixar spoke. The cold on his flesh grew sharper as the blackness grew thicker.

"Be gone from me!" Velixar cried, yanking down his arms. Six fingered hands ripped up from the black, some smaller than a child's, some as large as houses. Each one lunged to the sky, clutching and grabbing at the elves that circled above.

"Retreat!" one elf shouted, banking as black fingers tore through the air just before his mount. Another screamed as a hundred tiny hands enveloped him, crushing the life from his body. Dieredon clutched Sonowin's neck as a hand the size of a tree swung open-palmed at him. Sonowin spun, diving closer to the darkness and underneath the giant hand.

Cries of pain filled the night as more and more elves fell to the reaching black magic.

Dieredon held on tight, trusting his life to Sonowin. He scanned the battlefield while they whirled up and down, over one hand and then dancing away from another. Just as Sonowin pulled higher and higher into the air, outracing more than seven growing hands reaching up for them, the elf spotted two lone figures amid the sea of dead.

"Sonowin," he shouted to his steed. "There, you must get to them!"

The horse snorted, banked around, and dove straight for the approaching hands. A quick spiral avoided the first wave. Dieredon clutched his bow and held on for dear life, his eyes locking on the man in black who stood perfectly still, his arms at downward angles from his body. The rest of the elves were in full retreat. He was the only one left.

Qurrah watched Dieredon's approach with a gnawing fear in his chest. It seemed no hand could touch this one, the horse possessing dexterity beyond what any creature that size should have. Velixar showed no sign of being aware of their approach. His eyes had rolled back into his head as he controlled the multitude of magical hands.

"Be gone," Qurrah said, firing several pieces of bone. All pieces missed. He tried to cast another hemorrhage spell but the words felt heavy and drunk on his tongue. His mind ached, his chest heaved, and when the spell finished it created nothing but a wound the size of an arrowhead in the side of Sonowin.

"Master, defend yourself!" Qurrah shouted as loud as he could. Still nothing. More and more hands curled in, surrounding Dieredon and Sonowin in a magical maelstrom, yet still they came.

"Fly, Sonowin," the elf shouted. "Fly safe!"

Dieredon leapt from Sonowin's back, the blades on his bow gleaming. He fell through the air, the long spike on the bottom aimed directly for Velixar's head.

"Master!" Qurrah shouted again, shoving his body against Velixar's. His concentration broken, Velixar lost his control of the black fog. The darkness swirled inward as if Velixar were the center of a giant drain. The blackness filled him, surrounded him, and consumed him. When all returned, and Dieredon was about to land, a wave of pure sound and energy rippled outward. Velixar was waking, and he was angry.

The wave sent Qurrah crashing against a giant undead man still wearing rusted platemail. The collision blasted the air from his lungs. When he hit the ground, stars filled his vision. Dieredon fought but could not resist that same wave of power. The point of his blade halted a foot from the top of the black hood before he flew back. In the distance, Qurrah watched his master glaring at the damned elf who had fallen like a mad man.

"Scoutmaster," Velixar growled, his voice deep and dark like an ancient daemon of old. "Twice you have looked upon me and lived. No more."

Dieredon twirled his bow, his face calm and emotionless.

"Too many have died at your hand. What life you have ends tonight."

Velixar roared, a sound that made Qurrah shiver and avert his eyes. His master's back was to him, so he could not see the face that Dieredon saw, which was full of rotted skin and crawling, feasting things.

Suddenly Dieredon pulled back. The blades in his bow snapped inward.

"Arrows cannot hurt me," Velixar mocked. "They did not the first time. Why do you hope so now?"

"Because these arrows are different."

He fired three at once, all burying deep into Velixar's chest. The man in black screamed as the sacred water burned his skin. He fell to one knee and vomited a pile of white flesh and maggots.

"You will suffer," he gasped. "For ages, I will make you suffer."

"Try it," said Dieredon.

Two more arrows flew, but they halted in mid-air. Velixar stood, his hand outstretched, gripping the projectiles with his mind. The elf fired two more volleys but all the arrows froze beside the others.

"Fool," Velixar hissed. At once, the arrows turned and resumed their flight, straight at Dieredon. The elf dove, rolling underneath the barrage. Not an arrow had hit earth before the elf tucked his feet and kicked. The blades sprang from his bow. He crossed the distance between the two in a heartbeat.

Velixar accepted a stab deep into his chest. A pale hand grabbed Dieredon's throat, its grip iron and its flesh ice.

"It will be painful," Velixar said. Vile magic swirled about his hand, pouring into Dieredon's neck. The blood in his veins clotted and thickened.

A toss of his hand and the elf flew through the air. He rolled across the ground without the usual grace he had shown in combat.

Qurrah glanced about, paralyzed with fear. The remaining elves were returning, deadly and furious, and the darkness that had protected them was gone.

"Do you feel it?" Velixar said, stalking over to the dying elf. "The blood in your throat is clotting. Your mind will starve and your heart will burst trying to force blood through."

He knew he should speak. He had to warn master. But he could not open his mouth. He could not move. The pegasi were closer. They were readying their bows. He had to speak!

"Can you feel it?" the man in black asked. "Can you feel your heart shudder and throb? Here, let me help your pain."

Dieredon lay on his back, staring up at him. His chest was a mess of pain, his mind light and dizzy. As Velixar reached down, his maggoty face smiling and his hand dripping unholy magic, a wave of arrows rained upon him. Five buried into Velixar's back. Six more found his legs and arms. He arched and shrieked as the blessed water seared his wretched body.

Dieredon staggered to his feet, his bow still in his hands. The man in black reached around and tore out the arrows from his body. Still no blood flowed.

"My name is Dieredon," the elf gasped. "Know it before I send you to the abyss."

He fired two arrows, one for each eye. They shattered into fire, and finally blood did flow. It ran down the dead flesh and bone that was his face, over his black robes, and pooled in the grass below. He fell prone, still screaming his anger and fury. For five hundred years he had walked the land of Dezrel. All that time, all those killings, and this was how he would fail.

"Karak!" he shouted, all his power fleeing him. His undead minions collapsed, their souls released. The gates to the abyss opened before his eyes, and he felt the pull on his soul. The dark fire already burned. He saw the face of his master, and the sick grin there horrified him.

"I will not die!" he shrieked. "I will not die!"

His flesh burned in fire, his bones blew away as dust on the wind, and only an empty robe remained of the being that was Velixar. Yet, still haunting the wind, was his final cry, a promise to the world of Dezrel.

"I will not die!"

17

Miles away, Harruq awoke screaming. Aurelia rushed to his side as he curled into a ball, shuddering frantically.

"He's dead," he said. Cold sweat covered his body. Remnants of his nightmare floated before his eyes, the icy voice of Velixar rolling over him in his vengeful fury. All he'd known, all he'd ever loved, was dead and gone. Only Karak had remained, furious at the loss. Through it all, one single fact pulsed as an undeniable truth.

"Velixar," Harruq said, clutching Aurelia's hands and sighing with a mixture of relief and terror. "He's dead. I'm free."

Aurelia kissed his forehead as the half-orc drifted back to sleep, still overcome with his exhaustion. To her eyes, it seemed he slept far better than he had before.

Qurrah did not know what to say or do as he watched his master die. His entire world had just come crashing down in the darkness. Above him were more than fifty elves, each one eager to bury an arrow in his back.

"Harruq," he said, crawling amid the bodies. He desperately hoped none would spot him. He reached a large stinking corpse lying on its back with a golden arrow in its forehead. Qurrah shoved the cadaver onto its side, curled underneath, and then let it fall atop him. The weight crushed his fragile body and the smell was awful, but it was his only cover. Miserable, he hid there, quietly whispering.

"Where are you, Harruq?" he said, his face buried into the dirt. His tears fell to the grass. "Harruq, I need you. Where are you?"

Then he heard talking and shut his mouth.

"Are you alright, Dieredon?" an elf asked. The scoutmaster nodded, leaning heavily on his bow.

"I will be fine. His magic left my body upon his death."

A neigh brought his attention upward. Sonowin landed next to him, her white hair stained red in places. She nuzzled the elf and snorted something.

"You worry too much, old girl," Dieredon said, his voice cracking several times. He patted her once and then turned to the elf standing nearby. "How many did we lose?"

"Half. We paid dearly to kill this man."

"A heavy price," Dieredon said, gingerly climbing atop Sonowin. "Heavy, but well worth its weight in blood. A great evil has left this land. Let us return to Woodhaven, for this place of death turns my mouth sour."

The two took to the air and joined the other survivors. They did not try to locate their dead among the hundreds of other rotting bodies. Instead, a few elves flew low and scattered firestones, small pebbles that burst into flame upon landing. Grass and bodies ignited, and the battlefield rapidly swelled into a giant funeral pyre.

Qurrah crawled out from underneath the body as flames erupted all around him. Everywhere he looked, he saw embers and corpses. He spotted the robes of Velixar and ran to them. He picked them up and shook them, furious that no body remained.

"You lied to me, Velixar," Qurrah said. "You said you were eternal. You said you held the power of a god. But you lied. You are nothing but dust."

Surrounded by fire and death, the half-orc stripped naked of his rags and donned the robes of his former master. Despite all the arrows and heat, they seemed in perfect condition. Even the stain of blood was already fading. Qurrah held the side of the hood to his mouth and coughed as the smoke grew ever thicker.

"Goodbye, Velixar," he said. Then he chose a direction and staggered away. Slowly, and with a few wide curves through the carnage, he found a way out. He huddled the black robes tighter about his thin body, relishing the soft feel and perfect fit. Smoke clogged his lungs, but the stinking waves of it were lessening the farther he walked.

"Where are you, brother?" Qurrah asked once he could breathe freely. In the dark before the dawn, it seemed he would receive no answer.

At last, he could travel no more. He had no food, no destination, and no company. His limbs were weak and his head throbbed. To his knees he slumped, and he let time pass and his strength return, while his mind rumaged for ideas of how to proceed.

⋈⋈

While the sun was still a sliver peeking over the horizon, Aurelia shook Harruq's shoulders to wake him. She then sat back and put her hands to her forehead while the half-orc tried to remember where he was.

"Can you find him?" Harruq asked her, realizing what she was doing. He sat on his rear and began readjusting his armor to his more slender frame.

"In time," she said. "I have met him only once, but I doubt there are any like him. Stay quiet and be patient."

Her mind was a net, and she cast it further and further out, scanning the rolling hills and the plains beyond.

"Found him," she whispered.

⋈⋈

A blue portal ripped through the air before Qurrah, beckoning him. He looked through but saw only mists and distorted landscape. Seeing nothing to lose, he got to his feet and stepped inside. He felt the sensation of traveling a great distance yet his mind insisted he had taken only a single step. He could see the orange glow of the great pyre several miles away.

"Brother!" Harruq cried, wrapping him in a hug. Qurrah endured it, keeping his hands at his sides. "I was so worried about you!"

"Velixar is dead," Qurrah said, eyeing Aurelia warily.

"We know," the elf said. "It is well to meet you again, Qurrah."

Qurrah stepped back from his brother, and Aurelia noticed his robes and frowned.

"You should have left them. He was an evil man. Following in his footsteps will lead to a similar fate."

The half-orc said nothing. For a moment all three glanced about, the atmosphere akin to air before a thunderstorm. Qurrah broke the silence.

"Woodhaven is behind us," he said. "I have made mistakes, as has my brother. I saw you leave with him, and I know you sacrificed much to protect him. For this, I thank you. All I ask is that we speak naught of this again. If we are to travel together, it is my only wish."

"A wish gladly granted," Aurelia said, a tiny smile finally cracking free. "So where is it we should go?"

Qurrah glanced at his brother and shrugged.

"The only homes we have known are Woodhaven and Veldaren. I doubt either will gladly accept us."

"I have never been to Veldaren," Aurelia said. "Although I have heard it is beautiful, in its own way. I can get us inside, if all you fear are the gate guards. The edict to banish elves is foolish, anyway. After the casualties he took in Woodhaven, the king should be forced to revoke it lest any human villages be attacked."

"I wouldn't mind going back home," Harruq said. "Sound good to you, Qurrah?"

"Wherever you two go, I will follow," he answered.

"Settled then," Aurelia said. "You two are going to have to play along when we get there, though." She glanced at the sky, which was still speckled with stars even though dawn fast approached. "We'll wait until morning. I could use a bit more sleep."

She walked away, cast a levitation spell upon herself, and then settled in for sleep hovering an inch above the grass.

"Odd girl," Qurrah whispered. Harruq forced a laugh. To Qurrah's eyes, he looked exhausted, and the shrinking of his muscles was glaring.

"I'm sorry I left you there at Woodhaven," Harruq said. "And I'm sorry you were alone when Velixar died. How did it happen?"

"Elves came and attacked. No apologies are necessary, Harruq. All is forgiven."

"No, it's not all forgiven," he said, grabbing his brother's shoulders. "I can see it in your eyes. Please understand. I would have given anything to be there with you."

Qurrah's bloodshot eyes lost their rage and sorrow.

"But you weren't." His voice lowered, as if he were afraid Aurelia would hear. "You abandoned me for her. You left me, still wounded and alone. And I know what you did, brother. You turned against Velixar. You denied the gifts he gave you."

"He's gone," Harruq said. "And I want that strength no more. We are not his slaves."

"We were his disciples."

"We were his weapons!" Harruq shouted. He glanced back at Aurelia and held back a curse.

"Weapons," he said again, his voice an angry whisper. "Nothing more."

"If that is your belief," Qurrah said, settling down upon the grass. "But don't forget the blood on your hands. You killed more than I, brother. Now leave me be. The night has been long, and I need to rest."

Harruq let Qurrah sleep in the flattened grass by the fireside. As for him, he sat between Aurelia and Qurrah, glancing back and forth between the two.

"I can love them both," he repeated, though seeing the robes Qurrah wore, he wondered how long before that love split to one or the other.

The Weight of Blood

EPILOGUE

Far away, ash floated on a cold breeze, sucked into a forgotten cavern within a chasm feared by orcs and goblins. On the damp floor it fell, coalescing into a black muck, which stirred by unseen and unfelt winds. Here a bone poked up from the filth, there a fingernail. Floating above, transfixed in patient stasis, a soul awaiting a host, shone two crimson eyes.

A note from the Author:

I never set out to write a dark fantasy. I had two characters in my head, troubled half-orcs without home or family and whose decisions would one day bathe a world with war. To tell their story I had to start at the beginning, and the beginning is not kind. Reading some letters and reviews, I've seen just how dark I've gone.

What you have just read is a slight alteration from my original manuscript. I have not changed the brothers' actions. Instead, I have tried to show a bit more into their thoughts, their hearts, and their souls. I have had people call Harruq and Qurrah evil. Perhaps you agree. Much of what they have done certainly is evil. I will not sit here and justify the deaths of children, and to do so would paint me a psychopath and my characters sick beings.

I view Velixar as sort of a recruiter, the kind of man who'd be right at home at a Nazi rally filling confused kids with bigotry, anger, and murder. He is gone, for now anyway, and in The Cost of Betrayal these two brothers will get a chance to live on their own. For once Harruq has not only felt regret but done something about it. For once Qurrah has seen that the darkness he follows is not the absolute power it claims to be.

This Half-Orc Series is a story of redemption. I will not tell it in just one book, not even in two or three. People will die, and I will break the hearts of my beloved creations. If you've read this far and enjoyed it, I welcome you to continue along with me, as well as thank you for your readership. Your time is precious, dear reader, and I couldn't be happier knowing you spent it with me.

If you'd like to email me for any reason, ask questions or give suggestions, you can contact me at ddalglish@yahoo.com. Also, I'd like to give a quick thank you to Peter Ortiz, who did my stunning cover art. You

can view more of his wonderful drawings at
http://standalone-complex.deviantart.com/.

Hope you had fun. Hope you were entertained. Most of all, I hope for a brief moment you forgot your own world and got lost in mine.

David Dalglish

CPSIA information can be obtained
at www.ICGtesting.com
Printed in the USA
LVOW07s1409261016
510381LV00001B/18/P

9 781450 574488